I0590157

He Opened His Eyes and it was Dark

By: R. R. Griffin

Paul Bunyan Publishing Co.

2025

Author's Forward:

Dear Reader,

I have enjoyed (most of) the 13-year process that it has taken me to write this book and I hope that it resonates with you and leaves you thinking about the world around you and the part that you can play in it. To that end, I feel the need to start with a disclaimer. This book is a call to action in so many ways; a call to look at the toll that the stagnation of the status quo is already taking on the world around us, a call to think about the ways in which that stagnation is the product of both intentional and unintentional actions by many powers that be, and a call to think about the way in which you interact with the world around you; so as not to join the mind-numbing march towards the world created on these pages.

While it is fully written with the intent to inspire people to think about how they can affect change (even in small ways), this book is ABSOLUTELY NOT a call for violence or to allow hatred and despair to overwhelm that which makes us good. It is not a manifesto written to make violent people feel justified, but rather a harsh and sobering look at what the world very well may look like if apathy by ordinary people and indifference by people in power continue to allow the faults in our systems to go unchecked. My aim is to make you, Dear Reader, feel some of the pain the characters feel in this all-too-possible future. Compassion and sympathy are the enemy of the callous indifference that keeps our world from becoming the best that it can be.

It is my belief, at the time of this publication, that the world I have created in this story is still not a foredrawn conclusion we will inevitably see come to pass. I still believe that there are civil and institutional means that can be used to avert the bleak world you are about to enter. My hope is that when you read this, it inspires some part of you to seek out the ways in which you can help make sure this stays a work of fiction.

My final plea, Dear Reader, is that (both inside the covers of this book and in your lives) you never give in to the darkness. Even with everything going wrong in the world, it is still a beautiful and bittersweet place that is better for you being in it.

I hope you enjoy this book,

-R. R. Griffin

Acknowledgements:

The first thank you goes to Jacob Sorich for his incredible help in bringing this story to life. Jacob is the author of two historical books about Butte, Montana (one of the most interesting towns you have probably never heard of) and helped immensely by stepping in and writing the backbones of many of the chapters in the novel's second act. There are several memorable scenes that Jacob breathed to life on the page. Jake, I will be forever grateful for your help.

The second thank you goes to Wes Choc for lending his penchant for grammar and punctuation to the earliest versions (I was nowhere near the writer I am today when I started writing this novel in 2012) of the first dozen or so chapters. Wes is the author of his own unique memoir, as well as having written a biography and several other works.

A major thank you is in order for my family and friends (most of all my parents and my friend Susan). I went through many phases throughout the time it took me to write this (some ups, many downs, addiction, mental health concerns, nearly 2 years of homelessness) and I know it would have been easy for all of you to give up hope that I could get through it. I appreciate that you held out hope.

A special thank you to my lifelong friend Owen. Not just for being the last one trying to help me out of the impossible downward spiral I had allowed my life to become, but also for being a voracious reader of cool and interesting literature. When I set out to write this, I aimed for the very high bar of writing a book that you would enjoy reading–I do hope that it has hit that mark.

A final thank you to you, Dear Reader. Don't let anyone tell you books are lame. Without you, we may never hear the best stories that humanity has to offer.

A story in three acts:

Act 1:

Chapters 1-15

Act 2:

Chapters 16-28

Act 3:

Chapters 29-34

Chapter 1

He opened his eyes and it was dark. Truth be told, it was always dark. It didn't seem to matter what time of the year it was, a person could never guess exactly what any season would look like-considering the seasons had grown nearly interchange-able. He took a deep breath which induced a raspy smokers cough, a cough that he had already developed though still a young man in his 20's. He threw off his aging and worn-out wool blanket.

The shock of the cold hit him immediately. The power must be cut off again. He couldn't help but think 'Clearly the shitbrains that ration the power are useless.' Knowing there was no reason to try, he got out of bed and walked over to his desk to flick his lamp switch. It was a whole lot of nothing; of course it was nothing, a whole lot of freezing his balls off nothing. Those idiots at the power station were even dumber than the people who attended his middle management school. 'They are *all* useless,' he thought.

He pulled open the top drawer of his desk and fumbled around for a pack of cigarettes. His hand came to rest on his father's revolver—he didn't know why he kept it, undoubtedly, he could be arrested for having it. Shortly after coming to school, massive hunger protests had broken out and there were small groups of people that tried to use violence (many of which were armed) to force change. In a way they did. After that, you had to be a member of the current administration to own any kind of weapon and they arrested thousands on suspicion alone. His father was a pacifist when he spoke and had already died long before the new laws, so nobody had even asked Richard.

He kept it out of nostalgia for his father. His father's revolver and his father's golden Swiss pocket watch were the only two remnants that he had left of him.

He found his cigarettes in the clutter; so, pushing both worry and sentiment aside, he struck a match (he was happy enough to use a lighter when he was away from his dorm, but he liked the feel of using matches when he was in his room) and lit his first cigarette.

There was an immediate change in his demeanor, smoke filled his lungs, and the discontent of the ball freezing cold was lifted. After a few more intense drags to heat the cigarette up, he put it to the wick of a candle on his desk in order to light it.

The dim light of the candle lit his wiry body. He stood about six foot two inches and, though he was not skeletally skinny, was not half the mass of the majority of the fat-ass dragoons he encountered daily.

He walked over to his window to check the weather. Yesterday, it had been a temperate 65 degrees. Today it was snowing dark sooty snow. It was snowing and the regulators shut off the power.

Having already sucked most of his first cigarette down in a dozen massive inhales, he lit another off of it and inhaled deeply-- provoking the raspy cough that could only be relieved by more smoke in his lungs. In order to alleviate his cough, he put the cigarette back to his lips and inhaled more shallowly this time-- immediate relief. Students by general rule were not allowed to smoke in their dormitories, but after a few years he had completely given up on following any supposed guidelines. Most days he didn't even know why he stayed at the dismal college surrounded by brainless drones who drifted from gold star to gold star.

It felt like he could barely remember a time when work was graded on anything but an acceptable (check mark) or an unacceptable (red X), but (having been at the college for more years than he should) he actually could. He seemed to know a lot of things in the back of his mind that nobody else had any recollection of. This could possibly be accounted for by the fact that he was older than many of the students in their last year, but a part of him felt like it was because they either didn't want to or *couldn't* remember.

'No,' he thought with a slight hint of sympathy, 'they didn't remember because they didn't know any better.'

His cigarette was nearly finished. He looked around the room. On his ratty bed there were several open books; not the books about functioning that were the required school reading, but *actual* books. His mind flashed back to the rosewood handle of the revolver that lay in his drawer. The books wouldn't matter on their own, he would just go down somewhere in a school file for being one of *those* weirdos—it was the revolver that would really get him into trouble. Most of the books had come from his father's library and were now considered unproductive to own because they weren't dedicated to supporting the system, but he loved them and so far as he could tell they were the only thing that loved him back. His best love in the world was a set of damned books.

In the window the dim light of the candle showed his reflection. He hadn't shaved for at least a week and his messy hair gave him a haggard look that scared his clean-cut rank and file peers. That they would be considered "*peers*" was a fucking joke. He reached down to scratch his thigh and realized that the cold had seeped through his worn-out boxer underwear and had reduced his penis to infant size, so he looked around for his well-worn denim jeans. His eyes came to rest on a lone earring lying on the floor.

He wished she could be here to see his baby dick, that way she might not come back. Every few nights Janis rapped on his door. Drunk as he (undoubtedly) always was, he always let her in.

She was one of the biggest piles of slogan flinging shit at the college. She was an expert in functionality classes. She grasp-ed the notion of how to be a shitbrain with extreme passion because she knew all the meaningless words to say at all the appropriate times. She was slated for an excellent middle management job in the department of efficiency monitoring.

The most fucked up thing, he thought, was that one day it would be *her* job to tell *him* that *he* was the shitbrain. Except it wouldn't be a "shitbrain", it would be "unproductive." He knew the only reason she came back night after night was that he wasn't a fat-ass dragoon like the rest of his "*peers.*"

His "*Peers*" were just a bunch of people who can memorize words for a few days so that they can get the check mark and then forget the information and move on.

He had eventually made a point of not actually talking to Janis when she knocked on his door for sex, half in the hopes that she would get bored with him and half so that he wouldn't get put

5

off by her bullshit-slogan-slinging personality. Half of him liked the mindless sexual energy she was always rampant with; the other half had to squelch the urge to vomit at the thought of her mindless obedience to a clearly derelict system.

Pulling on his jeans, jeans that had enough holes that he should justify buying a new pair, he found that he had the urge to pee.

He hated any time he had to use the communal bathroom in the dorm. Inevitably, every time he made the trip, he ran into some asshole that wanted to horse around and/or, God-forbid, strike up a conversation about some stupid happenstance that had recently happened to them. He never wanted to deal with either scenario. Still, he resigned himself to make the journey regardless of if he had to encounter either.

In complete darkness he stumbled down a long hallway, instinctively working his way to the restroom. Without any encounter, he pushed open the door. On his way to the urinal, he heard a sound that let him know someone else was in the bathroom.

'Fuck,' he thought.

He attempted to relieve his bladder as quickly as he possibly could, hoping with all his might that he wouldn't have to see anybody.

Mark came ambling out of a stall. He knew Mark's footsteps at once because Mark always shuffled. Mark had either noticed his shape in the darkness or heard the spattering of urine.

"Hullo, hullo," Mark called out as he passed the urinals.

He gave no response. He liked Mark, because Mark wasn't pretentious like most of the people around him. Still, Richard didn't want to talk at this point in the night.

The faint light from the window gave away Richard's shape. Mark stopped just short of the urinals and asked, "Is that Richard?"

"Hey man," is all that Richard replied.

Mark shuffled back and forth on his feet, waiting for Richard to say more. After a few moments he gave up and said, "Well, I guess I will see you later," then left without washing his hands.

The fact was, in Richard's mind, that Mark was actually very tolerable. There was something endearing about his naive optimism and he, like Richard, was one of the few people at their middle management college who wasn't nearly as round as they were tall. Richard stumbled through the darkness back to his room and couldn't help but smile, a smile inspired at the thought of Mark's decency and innocence.

The darkness gave way to the outline of his rotting door

juxtaposed against fresh cheap white paint covering the cracking wall that framed it. He made straight for his desk. With the regulators cutting the power so damn always, his father's golden Swiss pocket watch was the only reliable way to tell time.

He reached into the top drawer of his desk looking for the pocket watch and for the second time, his hand brushed the rosewood handle of the revolver momentarily before seizing on the heavy gold trinket. Quarter to five it read, that meant he had over five hours until his *Understanding Language* class. He wound the watch, set it back in the drawer, blew out his candle, walked over to his ratty bed, pulled his worn-out blanket over himself, and went back to sleep.

Chapter 2

She stood on the balcony of her father's mansion looking at the dull sunset. In her lifetime–the beauty of sunsets had continued to diminish, but it still never failed to give her a sense of warmth and home despite the fact that the sunsets had dulled. She was wearing an uncomfortable, but absolutely beautiful purple dress. Fancy dresses always made her feel elegant and that was fine enough most of the time, but the charm wore off more quick-ly on her than it seemed to wear off with the other women around her. Personally, she wanted to retire to her room and put on more comfortable clothes, but she knew her father would talk her ear off about it if she did.

Lately it seemed like he wanted her to be more and more

involved in meaningless conversations and chided her when she forgot details about things the important people she met had said.

Usually, she was pretty good about listening intently to what the people were talking about, mainly to tell her brother later on, but sorting out the details of seemingly identical important people got old. It frustrated her how similar they were, but most of them were at least kind to her face. She knew most of them were doting on her as a way to butter up to her father.

'Who wouldn't be nice to the 'elegant' daughter of a general?' she thought to herself, cynically. Now she was of age–the uninteresting, yet important people, were bringing their overly-dressed awkward sons to say the same disingenuous kind things to her.

The last few years she knew she had 'grown into herself.' Whenever she had a dress on and looked down at her body in a mirror, she could see how well it fit her newly developed figure.

In the past, dresses had always made her feel as if she was playing dress up. Her once fragile and awkward limbs now formed sleek and graceful shapes accented by bronzed lean muscles. Her short and, what she had always thought of as, a rectangular frame had developed curves and elongated. The change had caused every "important person" to parade a whole host of their mindless, but soon to be important, awkward sons in front of her. It was certainly not playing dress up anymore, she was expected to pick one of the boys and join the bureaucratic nightmare that was her father's world.

The awkward boys were seemingly well intentioned once they got done gawking at her chest and finally looked her in the eyes. Some of them even occasionally said things that interested her, but she could almost see the moisture leaking into their palms as they tried to pay attention to what she was saying. It never seemed to dawn on any of them that every time they took a little hormonal break to gawk at her body, she became less and less interested. By the end of the conversations, the boys were almost all as dull as the now fading sun.

For the last few weeks, it seemed like she couldn't stand in one place for a minute without her mind being flooded with thoughts. It was her brother. He moved out of their father's house shortly after he turned 18 and the last few years of keeping up with both of them, who had not spoken to each other since her brother moved, had become increasingly difficult. She knew her father was a sympathetic man. He, unlike most of the important people, seemed to be aware of the suffering within the city. Occasionally he would voice sympathy and concern to her and a few times he had been able to tell her about actual things he did to help people. Her brother wouldn't hear it, to him their father was just another cog in a broken machine.

It unsettled her to think, but she had to admit that as time went on, she seemed to agree with her brother more and more. At first, she had avidly defended their father to her brother and couldn't understand how he refused to see the good, but the more time she spent out in the city the more she knew how little her father was doing.

Ever since she had begun to venture out on her own, it had gotten worse. It was easy to see that buildings all over the city were beginning to crumble faster and faster and there was no concerted effort by her father or his party guests to do anything about it. They would all congratulate each other on the small things they did, as if they had somehow saved the world.

She remembered a time, not that long ago, when teams of construction workers filled the city by night to repair damages to buildings. Anymore, most buildings were just abandoned and left for squatters. What was worse was how the Citizen Watchers had come to fill the streets. When she first began exploring the city on her own, there had hardly been any of those violent and deranged men.

According to her brother, most of the Citizen Watchers were soldiers or police kicked out of the military or the police for breaking rules. Insubordination or murdering innocents, it didn't matter. These violent maniacs were all given a paycheck and turned loose on citizens.

It was hardly fair for her to worry about her brother's safety considering her newest pastime of ambushing the unsuspecting predators that made up the Citizen's Watch. She had even had some close calls. One of the times, her successful ambush came down to the fact that the last of three men had hesitated for a second (probably out of shock at seeing his friends unconscious and writhing at the hands of a girl) and it was just long enough for her to hit him square in the chest.

A gasping vacuum sound croaked out of his throat before collapsing into a ball like his friends. Citizen Watchers were not allowed to carry guns-which was far more than could be said of her brother's targets. He had recently told her about his plans to hold up government convoys carrying food to the rich districts in order to drive them into poor districts to abandon for the people of the area to raid.

The thought of her brother being shot or captured terrified her. He had always told her that, "If something were to happen, at least it would mean something."

She didn't buy it; he was her brother and what he was doing was dangerous. He didn't just want it to mean something; it was the thrill of the defiance that also had gotten ahold of him. Still, she couldn't help but see the hypocrisy behind her worry.

Her head flashed back to her immediate world and she

realized that she had left the party over an hour ago. Hoping that her father had been too preoccupied with conversation, or perhaps that he had gotten drunk, she walked steadily on her slender heels back to the dining room. She paused momentarily in front of the mirror outside of the dining room door. Looking at herself up and down, slowly inspecting: first her makeup, then her hair, and finally her dress. She was still sufficiently "elegant", so she went in.

Chapter 3

Noise from the hallway woke him. Their laughter pierced the inch of rotting wood that was his door. Two or three of the dragoons must have found something astoundingly funny. It was a shrill type of laughter which was often heard when groups of prepubescent boys make some kind of distasteful joke.

Judging by the dim ray of light coming from his window, it must be nearing ten o'clock. He considered for a moment shrugging off his *Understanding Language* class (he did have a habit of not showing up for it), but he was already awake and couldn't think of anything better to do. Resigning himself to another day of frustrated agony, he shrugged off his worn-out blanket and made for his top drawer. Another cigarette. The refreshing smoke filled his lungs as he sank into his hardwood chair and fished through the mess of papers on his desk.

It was a little difficult to see, so he flipped the switch on the lamp on his desk. He was quite surprised that it actually worked. He also turned on his father's old computer and was shocked that that too turned on, he would give it a minute to fire up and see if there was somehow internet.

His school was actually in one of the least poor districts, so there was a time when he had first come to the school that internet outages were less common. He had heard hundreds of stories at the bar he frequented that the internet was now almost non-existent in any of the poorer districts. It was strange, when he was a kid, he could remember a time when a good portion of the population still had cell phones. Many were hand-me-downs and people had already started to get frustrated as the service got worse by the year, but now service was so unreliable that almost no one around him had one.

Richard eventually found the paper he was looking for. He had written it a few years back when his cynicism and discontentment took a more targeted outward approach. He wrote it when he still harbored some notion of spiting the institution.

It was a lofty response to the prompt: "Why is the word duty the most important word in the workforce?"

By writing a ridiculous response, he had thought, he would show them their monotonous arbitrary prompts meant absolutely nothing. He had fumed over the incredulous nature of such a question, 'how could an institution call *that* learning?' he had thought—he had been so idealistic back then.

Today's homework was the same prompt for the same class. He had a habit of failing his *Understanding Language* class with a glorious red X because he continued to turn in cynical, albeit well written, responses to prompts that were clearly meant to teach how to dehumanize the lowest class of worker...it was a middle management college, after all.

He read through his paper again. He had read it so many times that he had stopped counting. But every time he read it, he reveled in his own lofty defiance:

"On the subject of duty there are two principal properties that come to mind. The first property is most closely synonymous to the abstract notion of forced servitude. Duty is a word that the multitude stomachs in order to justify their misplaced motivation. This motivation is directly tied to the institution's necessity of thoughtless and compliant workers. Compliance, though equally relevant to the prompt, is by far less pivotal to the functionality of institutionalized society than the property of mindlessness.

Mindlessness therefore logically embodies the second

property of Duty. Duty is the inability to think, the crippling fear of decisions, and the euphoric feeling one comes to associate with ultimate obedience. Duty is akin to the function a dog carries out to its owner; the desire to be fed mixed with misplaced gratitude for the feeder. Duty is to the workforce what a collar is to a dog, the ability to be pulled in any direction at any point by its master. If duty is fully understood, in the mindless way it must be applied to benefit the workforce, it enables any cog of the machine to be utterly expendable at any point. Duty is the ability to be led off of a cliff at the command of any external force deemed superior. Walking off a cliff at the command of the institution is the utter fulfillment of the word duty."

Absent-mindedly, he reached back over to his top drawer, grabbed another cigarette and lit it. He inhaled deeply, the raspy cough temporarily spared him, and he exhaled with a chuckle. None of these professors, Richard thought happily, would ever understand. Instructors year after year came back with the same response, "Unproductive at the highest level, suggested disciplinary action."

Putting the cigarette to his lips, his mind wandered to why none of the suggested disciplinary actions ever happened. He had never even been reprimanded before. He wasn't sure, but his best guess was that the school didn't care if he failed as long as they got their check. Outside of being overly brooding, turning in passive aggressive papers, smoking in his dorm, and skipping classes—he never really bothered anyone. He could vaguely remember his father going on the occasional rant about how schools were now just businesses.

After his mother passed away, he was visited by a man in a tailored suit who explained that his parents had left him a decent amount of money. Though far richer than most of the people in the city, he was still relatively poor compared to many of his '*peers*'—most of whom were underachievers (something Richard *did* have in common with them) that came from very well-to-do-families who would end up getting jobs through their parents (something Richard certainly couldn't).

He had already signed up for this college, so the man said that the tuition would be paid for him without him having to do anything. On top of that, he would get a decent amount of money that he could pick up at a bank near his school once a month. He spent most of his monthly allowance on cigarettes and alcohol, both were actually extremely cheap in comparison to food, and he could just eat at the school if he spent too much.

Buying food had gotten really expensive around the time he came to the college. When he was younger, there were still grocery stores and even though many people had already relied on rations—families with the means could still reasonably choose the food they prepared and ate. Richard didn't know exactly why, but at some point, the government had switched over to a system where rations were allocated based on a person's job in fixed amounts rather than being purchased from a store with the money people earned. What was more confusing was that the rations system hadn't replaced or even reduced the amount of money people earned, to him it seemed more like a matter of control than anything.

Some types of food were still sold for money. Sugary or fatty treats were available at the commissaries that sold cigarettes and alcohol. The system also allowed for a version of restaurants, though most were little more than bars which also happened to offer some type of hot slop if a person had the money to pay. It had been explained to him by the owner of the bar that he regularly frequented that most of the slop-restaurants traded liquor to people for their rations in order to acquire the food to make the slop they sold. The owner had told him that between licensing and distribution fees, food was prohibitively expensive whereas alcohol was subsidized to allow it to be sold cheaply.

There were times that Richard considered the elements of his hypocrisy–sitting around his paid-for dorm, judging the whole messed up system despite the comfort that money in his pocket and school provided meals offered; but every time he did, he had no solution as to what to do. Just packing up and leaving wasn't really an option because he had nowhere to go. Mark was his only friend, and Richard didn't want to leave him; Richard wasn't left with any of his parents' friend's contact information; and at no point in his entire schooling had teachers taught him much about what was even outside the city. The entire system was designed to trap you in.

Richard hated anytime he had to leave his room, but he especially loathed crossing the grounds risking unwanted encounters. The snow from the evening was already melting and the temperature was up from a few hours ago by nearly thirty degrees. "The Power regulators who cut power when a cold front comes in must run the weather too," he thought. It seemed as if the world could never get anything right.

He walked by a row of trees whose leaves were an odd mixture of gray and green; the trees brought a visceral memory to his mind.

He remembered nearly twenty years ago, walking hand and hand with his mother and father down an avenue with a similar row of trees. He could remember that trees were almost completely green when he was young. Not the gray-green they had become, just green. He had an idea (not a definitive answer) as to why trees were now gray as well as green. It was most likely the same thing that made the sky so frequently dark and the weather so erratic. He couldn't exactly explain the details of why the trees were dying because his father had been the only one to talk about it and that was many years ago. Nobody else had ever even *talked* to him about it since, let alone tried to explain it. In the back of his mind, he knew that it had to be that the erratic weather was taking its toll.

His father had also told him of a time, long before he was born, when the sky was a vivid shade of blue on a clear day. Even as a small child he could never remember the sky being more than a light shade of blue imposed in the background of gray-black smog and soot. The idea that there was a world nicer than his that he barely missed always stirred up both feelings of sadness and anger.

He snapped out of his memory and saw a familiar person coming in the opposite direction. Gregory was walking towards him on the sidewalk. Gregory did not seem like a shitbrain, but he did have a consistent mean streak. Richard had seen him flare up in a testosterone induced rage and throw a kid through a classroom door a few weeks ago.

As mean as Gregory could be, he seemed to give Richard some type of distance. Richard made a point never to engage Gregory in the slightest (more out of fear than cunning) and then, for the most part, Gregory acted as though Richard didn't exist. As far as Richard was concerned, it was a spectacular arrangement.

It was strange, but Richard had a suspicion that Gregory wasn't actually like the rest of the students who made up the everyday drudge that was middle management college. He even went so far as to speculate that Gregory might have the same frustrations that he himself did. Somewhere behind Gregory's testosterone induced rage was a sort of intelligent spark. Richard couldn't identify exactly where this observation came from, but he instinctively noticed there was something more calculated behind Gregory's actions than the other people guffawing down the halls. He even went so far as to suspect that the reason Gregory never troubled him was because Gregory knew that Richard was also not like the rest of the students. Frustration or not, Gregory was still one mean bastard.

Even with his speculation that Gregory was just frustrated in the same way he was, an irrational fear overtook Richard's mind. The urge to pivot and run in the opposite direction surged through him, yet he was captivated by Gregory's brutish size and menacing aura. Seconds before they were to pass each other he inhaled deeply and held his breath. The only acknowledgement given by the giant was a small yet seemingly knowing nod. In his fear and surprise, Richard barely nodded back.

Holding his breath as long as he could and walking as fast as he could, he tried to put space between himself and the giant who was Gregory. Once Richard felt he was a satisfactory distance from Gregory he let out his breath and a coughing fit immediately ensued.

Chapter 4

He was drunk. He was close-one-eye-just-to-see-straight-drunk. All he could hear over the dull communal murmur of the pub was Mark's silly laugh. Mark wasn't clearly visible unless he had one eye closed and every time Richard turned to look in Mark's direction the world started to spin. Though, guessing by the laughter, Richard was almost positive that Mark was talking to Old Dirge.

Old Dirge was a ragged old man who had been wandering the streets of the city since before Richard was born. According to Old Dirge, Old Dirge was a king. In fact, when he got drunk enough, he would rant and rave about how he came from a great line of kings. He had a loveable personality, but Old Dirge was one crazy bat.

Richard had always liked Old Dirge because before Old Dirge got too drunk, he would always talk about how the world used to be. Dirge had lived on the streets most of his adult life. Strangely, considering he could seem like a drunken lunatic at times, Old Dirge had a great memory. Before Old Dirge got into the drunken stupor he so often lived in, Dirge could spin a tale of the world as it used to be.

According to Old Dirge there was a time when entire buildings were full of fresh food that anybody could go get and that most people could afford. Even though he was young at the time, Old Dirge remembered going on trips to places with his parents. They would go in a nice car his father actually *owned*—to cross the countryside full of beautiful vibrantly green trees and sweeping meadows. Richard could never believe it, but Old Dirge even claimed that he had swam in the nearby lakes without breaking into a rash.

As the world spun around him while he nursed his drink, his mind began to wander back to his youth. It wasn't the untouched clean world that Dirge would talk into existence, but he had good times when he was young as well. The alcohol fueled his emotions as a vivid memory played in his head:

His mother's face was so bright and so beautiful. She held

his and his father's hand as they walked down the street basking in the (even at the time) rare sunshine on their way to a pool near their neighborhood. His father talked to her animatedly about days when they were younger. How they would throw Frisbees for hours on end in parks covered with neat green grass, how they would hike to the top of mountains in the summer to see the stars at their clearest, and how she would dress up in her finest clothes before they would eat like kings and dance the night away. In his memory, Richard could remember the stars in his mother's eyes when she and his father talked about their youth.

There was a slide at the pool. Richard remembered asking his father again and again to go down it with him and every time his father would. At the bottom, his mother would be waiting with her beaming face and her eyes shining like stars. His father would throw him in the air and he would splash down in the cool clear water. They laughed more that day than Richard could ever remember them laughing. Though Richard thought he must have been happy other times, that was the only time he could really remember *truly* being happy.

The memory had brought tears streaming down Richard's drunkenly sentimental face. He was too intoxicated to care if anybody saw, but nobody had.

The reason that nobody noticed was that a bar fight had broken out. A group of men in plaid flannels had started yelling racial slurs at a group of dark skinned Middle Eastern looking men in the matching "outsiders" uniforms they were required by law to wear. One of the "outsiders," who clearly had a hot temper and too much to drink, started yelling back. That was all the provocation the men in flannels needed to start thrashing him. Two of the flannel men held the outsider's arms while two others smashed their fists into his face. The other outsiders watched in fear. Even if they wanted to help, they were frozen in place by the reality that they most certainly would be blamed for the whole incident if they did anything to help their now unconscious friend. The men in flannel most likely would have flailed the outsider to death had Old Dirge not stumbled over and smashed his beer mug over one of their heads.

The other flannel men stopped and stared in surprise as the entire bar lit up with laughter. The flannel man who was hit made a violent move toward Old Dirge, but (even as drunk and as old as he was) Old Dirge slapped him straight in the face before the man could do any damage. The laughter doubled as the flannel man beamed red in embarrassment.

With an alcohol induced confidence, Old Dirge yelled at them; "That will teach you whistledicks to mind your own business."

"You know what?" Old Dirge asked, clearly playing to the now laughing bar as the flannel men stood there stunned.

"Go fuck yourselves!" He yelled with the utmost drunken enthusiasm, spit flying from emphasis. The whole bar exploded with laughter. Some of the drunker patrons, no doubt emboldened by Old Dirge, also threw their beer mugs at the stunned and now embarrassed flannel men; all of whom fled the scene.

Raising his arms in the air like a triumphant prize-fighter, Old Dirge began to parade around the bar. There was a chorus of "his drinks are on me!" sounding out from all corners. Richard, finding himself suddenly more sober, looked over at Mark who was in a fit of hysteria. Mark was usually skittish to the point of paranoia, but the alcohol he had drank had clearly given him liquid courage because he was laughing so hard that he could barely stop from choking. Old Dirge's free drinks extended to Richard as well as Mark and it wasn't long before Richard was so drunk that he *wished* he was *only* close-one-eye-to-see-straight drunk.

Old Dirge, though he had drank at least two beers to Richard's one, was still animatedly slurring his words, telling the story of how he was a king. Whenever Old Dirge got this drunk Richard took to calling him King Dirgery the Second.

King Dirgery the Second was quite an interesting man. Unlike Old Dirge who had only traveled the countryside in his father's car, King Dirgery had traveled the world in his father's airplane. He had eaten with princes in Persia, danced with duchesses in Denmark, thrown darts with the Royal Family in

Romania, copulated with courtesans in Cyprus, and prayed with the monks in Mongolia. In fact, there wasn't anything that King Dirgery hadn't done. If an eavesdropper had heard somebody once climbed Mount Everest, King Dirgery had climbed it with them. If they had heard of somebody who had rafted the Amazon, King Dirgery had rafted it too. There was simply nothing King Dirgery hadn't done; except of course anything, because King Dirgery didn't exist. King Dirgery was nothing but an old man who could remember riding through the countryside in a car that his father actually *owned*. He was simply an old man who had a great memory and a flair for dramatic storytelling.

Chapter 5

Richard fell down. The world was spinning so badly that the ground itself felt friendly. He would have liked to lay there forever, but he supposed that at some point he would have to abandon the ground, and his mind told him that he should do it sooner rather than later. Struggling to his feet was not his idea of comfort, but his dormitory was really only a few blocks from where he found himself lying. Staggering just to get up, he stepped in what he knew to be the right direction.

He fell again. This time, he barely caught himself and narrowly avoided smashing his forehead straight into the jagged pavement. It didn't even cross his mind that he was lucky to avoid the craigs and jags that were now on every sidewalk in the city.

Picking himself up off the ground for a second time he wandered, to the best of his abilities, back towards the dormitory that he so thoroughly resented.

In the past, Richard had wandered into alleys and dropped face down into an inebriated sleep–so he knew from experience that his skimpy mattress and worn-out blanket were more comfortable than broken pavement where he would sleep all night exposed to the (at times) toxic elements. Despite his resolution to make it back to his own bed, there was an alley a block and a half away that seemed equally inviting.

He stepped into the alley and began debating with himself between passing out where he was or making it all the way home. He fell again.

The strange thing was that this time he did not fall of his own accord. Or, at least he didn't think he did. His shoulders stung and his breath had been knocked out of him. Richard had had the wind knocked out of him before, but he wondered what the cause was this time. Rolling over and blinking into the darkness as he regained his breath, he realized that there was actually somebody else in the alley.

As he looked up, he saw a blurred face in front of him. The face belonged to (what he thought at least) was a fairly beautiful girl. She was probably in her mid-twenties and her face was void of the blank stare that was waxed onto so many of the faces he was used to seeing, a face that hadn't adopted a blank stare caused by a dull life of servitude and "duty." The girl stared at him for a while before asking him some type of question that he tried to hear and make sense of.

Though he didn't understand what she was saying (he had taken far too many people up on free drinks that night), he noticed her eyes. She had the same stars in her eyes that he remembered his mother having. Even as drunk as he was, he could see the eyes of a beautiful girl that had not yet been beaten down by the decay of society.

He mumbled something incoherently and tried getting to his feet. Her thin yet muscular arms wrapped around his midsection and he found himself successfully on his feet. He pointed in the direction he was going and slurred, "I'm only a few blocks away."

This time when she spoke, he did understand it, "I will help get you home safe. I'm sorry I crashed down on you, I mistook you to be a citizen watcher."

With one arm over her shoulder, they made their way back to his dorm. It was a somewhat painstaking trek, though the distance wasn't far. His spinning mind kept trying to lock onto a thought long enough to start a conversation about who she was or why she was here, but the alcohol had done a number on him. He labored in silence other than the occasional grunt when she would ask him if they were still going the right way.

Eventually the two found their way to the outside of his building. The effort of making it there had sobered him up enough to get out a crude, "Thanks for the help. I think I can make it upstairs."

He marched off like a man on a mission not to waste the last thirty seconds of composure he had left. She had said "you are welcome" and some other form of pleasantries as he walked away, but his whole focus was on getting the last forty feet to his bed.

Once he got there, he struggled to stay awake in order to remember her face. His memory was blurred by the innumerable pints of beer he had drank that evening, but a sweet smell lingered in his mind that he thought must have been her.

He struggled to remember what she had said to him after she crashed down on him in the alley. Something about the "citizen watchers" was all he could recall. When he was focused, he could recall her blurred beautiful face. Even though his recollection of her face was inhibited because he was extremely intoxicated, the stars he had seen in her eyes (even in the dim alley) were seared into his mind. No amount of alcohol could ever dim what he saw. It was the same thing he had seen in his mother's eyes when he was young.

As he lay in bed trying to hold on to the memory of the girl in the alleyway, his thoughts strayed to his mother. She had those stars in her eyes when he was younger, but most of his life they had gone out. He remembered what his mother had become:

It was several years after his father had been taken away. His mother had long lost any semblance of the vibrant beauty and sparkling radiance she once had. Worn, thin, and dismayed, she sat and stared out a window. Staring out the window was something she had taken as a pastime, vaguely looking as though she expected his father to round the corner of the street at any moment.

They had wanted for little. Richard had a vague understanding that their family had a fair amount of money, which was why they wanted for little-the little they did want was for his father to come back.

His mother was a hollow mess, a shadow in the distant wake of his father's exuberant confidence. A house once full of his life and energy sat in ruins of a long ago promise for a better and brighter world. Richard remembered some of what his father had believed in.

His father believed in a world full of parks with green grass, a world where everyone could have a decent life without working themselves to death, a world free of pollution and corruption. His father also very much believed in the stars that were once in his mother's eyes.

The intensity of his father's memory was a flame that stood out in the darkness of the world that he now found himself in, the flame haunted him by contrast. His memory was often a vigil in requiem for his father.

The second his father was taken away; his mother started to die. He was only a teenager, but he could see sadness had overtaken her heart and that his mother was already as good as dead. She was dead the moment a man, one he thought he had seen again, came and told her that her husband was never going to come back again.

He propped himself up on one elbow and focused on trying to remember his mother's eyes before the stars died in them. Strangely, the only eyes he could remember at the moment were the eyes of the beautiful girl who had crashed down on him in the alleyway. He reeled in thought, but the drunkenness overtook him, and he passed out into a deep sleep.

Chapter 6

King Dirgery the Second was at it again. The infamous event where he smashed a mug on the head of a person thrashing an 'outsider' had been told again and again and again; it had done nothing to curb Old Dirge's regal origins. He was no longer satisfied with just his line of kings. He added in saints, martyrs, pharaohs, half the book of kings, popes, chiefs, explorers, theologians, philosophers, emperors, every manor of scholar he could recollect, bards, sorcerers, and even a few gypsies. The incident had gone so far as to make him the supreme pontiff of the earth. According to the drunken King Dirgery the Second, there was no power other than God's which came before his own.

Before the free drinks they were still receiving had taken effect, Old Dirge told Richard one of the best things that Richard had ever heard. In Old Dirge's newfound glory, he remembered one of the things he used to do with his father that sounded more spectacular than anything Richard had heard Old Dirge talk about before.

Richard, having lived in the city his whole life, could never fully imagine the countryside in all its glorious colors. Richard was a young man who couldn't even imagine a country that was anything but broken, but Old Dirge seemed to be telling him something out of one of his banned novels he had from his father's library.

In what seemed to be a single breath, and with all the flair Old Dirge so easily mustered before he drank himself into a stupor, Old Dirge recalled with vivid detail:

"They were always cold mornings; not the seeping cold of today that makes you ache all the way down to the core of your bones, but a crisp, fresh and powerful bite. It was the kind of cold that made you feel so completely alive that the world seemed to be cut in vivid pixilation. The fresh snow on the ground was gilded with sparkling rays of piercing sunshine; sun that reflected off of snow that was so impossibly white and pure that it seemed as if it was the light of eons. If you could have seen that light, it would be unlike anything you have seen in your lifetime."

Old Dirge continued,

"If you could see crisp, white snow fall from the skies, the empty loneliness that has become the human experience in these times would be transmuted into a beautiful and lucid thing. Those moments when the snow fell were so harmonious that (even after all these years) it can easily drown out the feelings of this sea of non-existence.

My father would walk into the room bringing the promise of a day so simple and wonderful that all these years later the feeling of such uninhibited joy can't even be taken away from me. We would go and ski. I always felt a childish sense of anticipation of freedom that was found on the mountain even though the cold whipped at your face.

This was a time so far out of sight and out of mind that the decrepit world of pollution and decay we live in would have seemed like an alien existence."

Old Dirge took a long drink, looked off as he collected his thoughts, and then started back in,

"Imagine pure white snow that falls into a world of clear blue skies. It is such an unimaginable contrast to the acidic dark snow that falls these days that eats away at everything it touches. It was in that dreamlike world that my father would bring me up to ski. If one spent years in practice, a person could use two pieces of fiberglass to traverse down nearly impossible seeming terrain. At times even dropping distances the height of small buildings. My father was always so proud as he watched me traverse down all the faces of the mountain."

Old Dirge had heard his father say it many times, "At least my boy can ski."

He trailed off. In his seemingly breathless recollection, he had managed to finish a staggering amount of drinks. Three empty mugs sat in front of him and he was nearly done with a fourth. Once Old Dirge finished his story, he transformed in front of Richard. Eyes that moments before were alert became opaque. A chin that was usually set in lofty defiance resulting from too many years on the street sunk into a half jowl that indicated that he was ready to start telling anybody who would listen how he was the supreme pontiff of the world.

Richard knew Old Dirge well and regardless of how much Old Dirge would pontificate, Old Dirge's shoulders seemed to suggest that the shouldering of all the hardships of life were crushed under his alcohol-induced defeat.

King Dirgery the Second began to tell Richard how he had sailed the seven seas, but somewhere underneath the drunken ranting was the boy who had glided down mountains. Underneath the weight Old Dirge carried, there was still the kid whose father had everything he had ever wanted—his boy could ski.

Chapter 7

Janis rolled off of him. Richard felt dirty, dirtier than the dark acidic snow that had been falling steadily with all its soot and toxicity. His mind was squirming in self-loathing, so he got up from his bed to search for his worn-out boxers that had been flung (in drunken passion) into a corner of his room. Once he had his boxers on, he went to his drawer to grab a cigarette. The power was back on, so he was able to turn on his desk lamp.

He turned around to look at the beautifully bitchy face that he had come to loathe with every ounce of himself, save the lone fact that he was typically drunk and couldn't resist her vapid sexual energy. Before lighting the cigarette, he spit on the floor, a symbolic attempt to rid himself of the bubble gum flavor of her mouth.

His aura of loathing was completely lost on her as she got up and put her clothes on. Her face was smug with sexual satisfaction. He had the slight urge to gag at the thought that the smug shitbrain in front of him, who succeeded so fucking well at regurgitating every bullshit slogan she was ever fed, would someday tell him he was 'unproductive' and would force him to live a life like Old Dirge. A life on the street living from drunk night to drunk night punctuated only by ranting at anyone who would listen how he came from a great line of kings.

It was all he could do to stifle the impulse to scream at her and tell her how repulsive she was, to tell her how everything from the diseased snow to the shitbrains who couldn't figure out the power were all the product of her wonderful ability to spew whatever thoughtless slogan she needed to get her fucking 'productive' check mark. He looked at his half naked non-skeletally skinny body in the reflection of the window and noticed that he had crushed the cigarette in his clenched fist. Janis left the room, without so much as a backward glance. He pulled another cigarette out of the drawer and quickly lit it. Between the fervor he was in and the massive over-drag of his cigarette, he was hit with his raspy cough.

Richard paced back and forth, both drunk and unable to sleep. His self-loathing built to a breaking point as he thought over and over about how dirty he felt, covered by her vapid sexual energy. He felt he somehow needed to get out; get out of this dorm, get out of this school, get out of this diseased city. The stain of the latter seemed to have buried its way into the very depth of his soul.

Richard felt as if he had been lying out in the acidic snow, his anger reflecting the slow boils which bubbled up over anyone's skin that stayed for too long under its unnatural blanket. A sort of hopelessness overtook him and his anger subsided. It wasn't the first time he had felt this way; hopeless, angry, and resentful at the system of obedience.

Lighting another cigarette, he grabbed his denim pants that were overly worn and slid them over his thin wiry legs. Setting the cigarette down he grabbed a clean shirt off the floor and wrestled it over his head. Staring at his shaggy reflection in the window, he blindly rummaged through his dresser drawer. His mind didn't even register the feeling of brushing the rosewood handle that would *really* get him into trouble, before coming to rest on his golden pocket watch. The watch read 10:17 pm. Taking a huge drag off of the already almost extinguished cigarette, he looked for his sooty and acid-stained coat (that he always forgot to wash) in a pile of discarded clothes. Finding it, he shoved a half empty box of cigarettes into his pocket and left his room.

He stopped short in the front doorway of his dormitory. Suddenly he felt the desire for company, so he pivoted on the spot and made his way to Mark's room.

He tapped on Mark's door, lightly at first, and then loud enough that it would wake Mark. The door to Mark's room was in even worse shape than his own. In spots, the nightlight that Mark kept on (power allowing) for comfort could be seen through the thin wood.

Richard could hear the creek of the rusted down bed frame that Mark slept on. There were several occasions Richard had offered to buy Mark a new one, but Mark kept his bed for sentimental reasons. The frame was handed down from his grandmother and Mark kept it as a reminder of her.

Mark had told Richard all about his grandmother:

Mark had lived with her for most of his life. His grandmother was a woman who was typically harsh and crass to outsiders, but at the core she was a very nice person. She had taken Mark in when his parents, poor and starving, abandoned him on her doorstep. Mark had never fully processed why they left him, and his grandmother never told him why they never came back. Mark guessed that part of why his grandmother was so harsh sometimes had something to do with whatever had happened between her and his parents, but he had come to grips with not knowing.

His grandmother was generally a poor woman who often

had to go without food to make sure that Mark was taken care of. For Mark's whole life, she would tell him that someday he would go to school so he could grow up and be better than his father. Whenever she talked about Mark's father she donned an aura of bitter resentment. There were times where her comments about his father that he never knew had bothered Mark, but he was a good grandson and never wanted to upset her by asking questions about why she felt the way she did.

Sometimes she would go days on end without food while all Mark had was some chicken broth and a carrot or some noodles she would bring home from her part-time job at the rations office. To her credit, no matter how tired, hungry, and worn out she would get, she never once complained about Mark being a burden. She always encouraged Mark about how he would grow up and be better than his father.

The bed frame had belonged to her from the days of being married to his grandfather. Mark had figured out from the few times she would talk about him that he had run out on her and his mother when his mother was just a child. When Mark became old enough to sleep in an adult-sized bed, she gave her bed to him and bought a cot from an army surplus store.

As she got older, the harsh life started to get to her. She became prone to long bouts of sickness and her body withered into a hollowed out and leathered frame. Her sharp brown eyes began to glaze because chronic pain overtook her whole body.

Mark remembered the last day he had seen her happy. Shortly after he had graduated from '*The Industrial-Stocking Associated Corporation Primary School*', he came home from the job he had (which was just sweeping the floors of one of the many industrial plants in his neighborhood) to find her in a state of extreme excitement.

She had stopped off at the postal center and picked up a letter from the *Academy of Middle Management Company* that was addressed to Mark. Savoring the moment he slowly ran his finger down the first crisp white envelope he had ever seen. It was wholly unlike the flimsy yellow envelopes that most people had to buy.

His grandmother literally shook in anticipation as he read the letter:

Dear Marcus Spillman, we are pleased to inform you that you have been selected for an opening in our lower-middle management course. Details will be sent to you sometime in August and you will report for classes the third of September. Printed at the bottom in a type of ink that was made to look handwritten was their slogan, "Where the greatest duties are realized and fulfilled."— His grandmother literally let out a cry of joy.

She rushed down to the ration store and came back with the meal he only got once a year when it was his birthday; two pork tenderloins, corn on the cob, and cream of mushroom soup to which she added bits of ground beef.

In August the letter came, but so did a blizzard. For three days straight, the sky spit dark sooty snow, and the freezing temperatures froze the pipes that heated their apartment. It was either sometime during her walks to work through the snowy piles of polluted filth or the sleepless nights of terrible cold, but she caught pneumonia. Less than two weeks before he started on his new life of middle management, she spoke her last words to him "you have grown up a better man than your father" and then she died.

Richard heard Mark shuffle his feet across the floor before opening his door. When Mark opened the door and saw Richard, his face broke into a warm grin.

"Hullo, Hullo!" (Mark's trademark greeting)

Richard asked, "How is your evening going?"

"Good," Mark replied.

Richard angled his body sideways and began alternating from leg to leg. A few moments passed. Mark understood that Richard was about to ask him to come along for some of the debauchery that they both enjoyed. Richard turned and looked into Mark's brown eyes, "Would you want to take a walk down to

The Fellows Club on Fourth Street?"

Mark looked puzzled for a moment trying to think if he had ever been there. If he had, he knew for certain it had not been with Richard.

"Why would we go there?" Mark asked, with awkward curiosity.

"Does it matter?" replied Richard; not as a harsh retort, but because he didn't feel like explaining it in the dark hallway of their dormitory.

Mark replied jovially, "No, I guess not."

Chapter 8

They walked down a dimly lit street. Most of the once functional lampposts had long since had their bulbs broken by neighborhood kids roaming in packs. Kids who needed a cathartic outlet between their time in the run-down schools they had to attend and the time their parents came home from the ration center with whatever dinner their family's jobs could afford.

Fortunately, it had stopped snowing for the moment, and the weather seemed to be changing into something of a warm reprieve.

As they walked, Mark was anxious as well as winded because he was much shorter than Richard and had to almost jog just in order to keep up with Richard's strides. They had walked into a district of the city that Mark had never been in. Several times, Mark was on the verge of asking Richard if they could turn back and go to a more familiar bar, but Mark trusted Richard and followed him in good faith.

The district they found themselves in was arguably one of the poorest in the city. The lampposts would have been fairly tolerable had it not been for the apparent decay of the rest of the surrounding buildings. Most buildings had broken windows boarded up with rotting sheets of plywood. The plaster and paint were all peeling from the housing structures made of brick or concrete. The two of them passed several people huddled in doorways, people who were obviously out catching an amount of fresh air now that the toxic sooty snow had stopped.

Mark seemed on the edge of losing his nerve. Mark had grown up in a part of the city where people were poor and the buildings were dingy, but his neighborhood was not as bad as the one they were walking through. There were bricks that sat in heaps from where they had fallen off the buildings and it gave Mark an eerie feeling. It seemed as if they enshrined the poverty of the world around them.

This district, though not totally familiar, was not foreign to Richard. Richard had plenty of recollections of wandering into these types of poor districts in some of his late-night drunken wanderings. Even the first time Richard had walked down streets like these, he had a completely different reaction from his out of breath and anxiety-stricken companion.

Whenever Richard saw the terrible decay and poverty, he was always struck by a piercing hopelessness mixed with a desire to see justice. The struggles of the downtrodden had always threatened to overwhelm him with their seemingly irreversible natures. So many people lived such miserable lives that Richard felt there was no amount of money or cunning that could help them.

At some level he desperately believed that something *could* be done, things that his father used to talk about. In fact, his father had talked about it once at *The Fellows Club* that they were walking towards. Richard hadn't wanted to explain it to Mark in the dorm. A part of why he hadn't wanted to explain it was out of self-consciousness over having to reveal his feelings, but they were going to *The Fellow's Club* because he wanted to remember one of the last nights he saw his father. He hoped that it was something that would give him hope.

The decay of the neighborhood made Richard feel dirty, which caused his mind to focus back on Janis. He wanted to tell her off someday. He wanted to tell her that every piled brick, every broken light bulb, every poor person that he and Mark passed, and every last peel of paint on the buildings was her fucking fault. In his mind, it was her fault because she grasped how to be a shitbrain with extreme passion. Her mastery of the mindless slogans about duty to one's superiors, duty to her future employer, and duty to a god-forsaken country was to blame.

What kind of country was it where bricks sat as sad monuments to the sorrow, pain, and hunger that so many felt? Richard's mind flared. She had mastered the slogans about her duty to this rotting world so well that she would end up being a great instrument in keeping it rotting. Richard was so appalled by everything he saw he wanted to turn to Mark and take out his frustration by yelling.

Luckily, he didn't act on that impulse, because deep down Richard knew (even though Mark didn't see a lot of the things that Richard saw nor knew many of the things that Richard knew) that Mark was his closest friend in the world.

Richard had "friends" when he was growing up, but they weren't *really* friends. Yet for some odd reason, because most of them were nearly identical to the fat-ass dragoons at his school, they seemed more endearing to his memory. It was probably because they hadn't fully accepted their roles in the decaying society yet. As kids, his "*friends*" had not begun to take part in the great bureaucratic hierarchy that allowed buildings to crumble and kept people out on the street. Richard and his "*friends*" were all from families where finances were not a problem. He had fallen out of touch with them because they didn't care about the decaying world. It's one thing to be selfish, it's one thing to be rich, but if you are both, you are part of the problem.

Richard was younger then and hadn't seen as much of what the crumbling parts of the world were like. While his mother was still alive, he would never even have thought to wander through districts like these for fear of the people that inhabited them. Considering that he had grown up in a well-to-do community and that he looked like he did at the time, he would have been an easy target.

His parents' home was a two-story house with a small basement, but the house was decorated in reminiscence of the colonial era. Carved ashen oak wood banisters stood between the floors in the place of metal railings. When he was younger the décor of the house, with its intricate trim and hard wood floors, gave him a sense of comfort and security. The kind of delicate detail that gives a person impunity between themselves and the outside world. He could remember how his father had a way of delivering energy into the seemingly ancient ornamental wood which would enrapture anyone who was one of his father's guests.

Richard recalled, with as much clarity as possible, how his parents would sit around a polished kitchen table with strangers he was too young to get to know. They would drink wine and talk in passionate tones, broken periodically by laughter. Even though he was young, he could remember how his father seemed to emit a radiance into the room which captivated whoever was sitting at the table. Even as a child, he could recall the glow on his parents' guests' faces as they listened to his father speak.

Richard and Mark were coming out of the district with the decrepit buildings and broken streetlights into one similar to where Mark had come from. Most of the people in it were likely working for one of the industrial plants Mark used to sweep. Mark, though still breathing heavily, had lost some of the nervousness that he felt minutes before. This industrial district served as a barrier from the impoverished world they had just left and the well-off district that Richard grew up in. The Fellow's Club was only a few blocks away.

Chapter 9

They walked into the bar. The Fellow's club was a very large empty room with a short bar occupied by what could either be the regular crowd or the remnants of the evening. Mark, who was tired from the walk, was confused why Richard insisted on coming to this particular bar. Mark was confused because this place was far different from the usual rowdy places that he and Richard typically frequented. Mark was on the verge of asking Richard the millions of questions he had on the way over, but Richard strode purposefully toward the bar.

The barkeep was a squat man in his mid-forties who seemed to have avoided some of the wearing of age with a jovial face hiding a contempt for the world around him.

Richard stood stoically for a moment. Mark shuffled over to Richard's side and the barkeep came to take their orders.

"What's your poison?" asked the charismatic bartender.

Richard, who had a lot on his mind, answered; "Two pints of your regular beer and a dash of whiskey on the rocks for both of us."

Mark's face showed agreement. He *loved* whiskey--and even more, he loved Richard's *whiskey on the rocks*. Sipping it with Richard made the back of his throat burn as if he wanted to vomit, but there was almost a perverse pride in being able to sip something so repugnant.

Mark noticed something in Richard that was different from the usual sarcastic brooding. Richard seemed intent and focused. Changes in anything made Mark nervous. Richard sometimes said things that Mark didn't understand, but Mark always liked to hear Richard out (understanding or not). Mark did get the sense that Richard's face reflected something of the way that he himself looked when he talked about his 'Gran.'

Mark loved Richard in a strange way, Richard's thoughts intrigued him. His Gran, nor anybody else that he had met, ever said things the way Richard said them and Mark had certainly never heard thoughts the way Richard could (sometimes) put them. Mark wasn't afraid of Richard the same way he was afraid of almost everything. Normally Mark wondered what he was supposed to do, but Richard made it seem like he could just *be*...something had never experienced before.

The barkeep asked for payment in advance, so Richard dug into the pocket of his sooty acid-stained coat and pulled out a half dozen crumpled twenties. Richard shot the man a moderately condescending look to make sure he understood they could drink whatever they ordered the rest of the night without any more questions about whether or not they could pay. Despite the jovial nature of the bartender, he had an obvious look of shock that someone who looked like Richard had that amount of money which he could just pull out of his pocket. 'What a shit-brain,' Mark and Richard thought simultaneously—though they would never know it.

Mark was finally bursting with curiosity. "This is a pretty nice bar." Richard was staring off into space, so Mark got no response.

Mark raised his voice slightly, "But why *this* bar, Richard?"

Richard took a long pause, downed his whiskey in one long drink, took a swig off of his beer and looked at Mark. Mark was curious and nervous in equal measure.

Casually, Richard answered, "It's a nice bar, isn't it?"

Mark let the subject go. The fact was that Mark was good at letting the subject go, so good at it in fact that he was a great success in his Lower Middle-Management courses.

Richard, with all of his vaunted frustration, looked at Mark with a friendly gaze. Richard envied Mark in some ways. Mark had an ability to do shitbrain things without becoming one himself—a feat that was very impressive. Richard always felt comforted by his friend. So comforted in fact that he drank two more pints and downed an extra whiskey to Mark's one. Looking around, starting to feel the familiar drunkenness setting in and inspired by his father's memory, he decided to tell Mark about the time he remembered being at *The Fellows Club* when he was little:

"I sat at a table in this very room."

Richard paused for a moment to collect his thoughts before telling the full story as best as he could remember it.

"There were women dressed in finely made dresses and men in tailored suits. Everyone had a certain purposeful presence they seemed to want to project. The air was certainly tense, but not unfriendly. It was an air with a purpose. It was an air where people cared about being seen.

My mother was wearing her fanciest dress. She was regal and stunning, flashing a vibrant smile made warm by years of laugh lines and talking animatedly to everyone and anyone she saw; but something was hiding underneath the warmth. There was an underlying look of reserve and fear as if she somehow knew that some kind of tragedy would soon befall the people of the room.

As the feeling of the room became progressively more electric and excited, her smile became progressively more forced, and her eyes showed fear and doubt. Nobody, including my father, seemed to notice nor care. They continued talking in elated voices about things that went over my head because I was too young to comprehend what was being said.

The phrase 'for the people' stands out in my memory. Everyone wanted to make it clear that they had done *something*, in some way or another, related to '*the people*'. I don't exactly know who '*the people*' were, but it was an important topic of conversation."

Richard trailed off for a moment and looked around the nearly empty bar hall that had once hosted the people who obviously wanted to be seen and wanted to say all the right things to impress each other. The memory of the people in tailored suits and fancy dresses haunted the room in his mind like phantoms, barely to be remembered in the wake of the world he had now grown accustomed to.

People now went around day to day in their lives as if nothing mattered, most of them not even seeming alive. The poor people Richard and Mark had passed who inhabited the decrepit world they had to walk through to get to *The Fellows Club* were in such staunch contrast to the phantoms from that night he was recalling that he couldn't help but feel sorrow. Such recollections lived in his mind to be hopelessly smashed against the reality of the world that had come to be the one in which he lived.

Richard remembered the eyes and demeanors of the people at the party well, joyous and hopeful. His mother hadn't completely lost the stars in her eyes yet. But even as a teenager, he could tell that she knew that it may be the last night that she would ever be in a room full of suits and dresses.

Turning back to Mark, he resumed his memory:

"My father spoke to the entire room. There were others who had spoken about what they had done to benefit 'the people,' but my father was the last. My father was not only the last, he seemed like the most important."

Richard couldn't remember each and every word, but with the phantoms in the room his father's words came flooding back to him.

"My father was standing tall, knowing his words were about to reach a sympathetic audience."

Richard looked Mark straight in the face; "I can only

paraphrase, but I will tell you what he said to the best of my memory."

Richard began reciting what he recalled his father saying:

"I thank you for this honor. Years of hard work and dedication have brought us to this place. There isn't a single person in this room who hasn't tirelessly fought again and again for what we believe in. We have fought time and time again, but it isn't enough. Every day another child is put out onto the streets. Every day another family misses a meal because there isn't enough to go around. Every day, families all over this country have to decide between food and power. Yet, every day the very people who thrive off of poor people's suffering are better and better off. This world we live in is broken.

It is also a world where our means of living threatens to destroy the very world we live in. Already these *means* have caused unimaginable natural disasters. Disasters so bad that it is almost as if they are something you would read out of the bible! It is a world where greed is not only unpunished, but *celebrated*! It is a world full of pain and of suffering. A world where hope is all but impossible. It is a world where our institutions of learning have fallen to the highest bidder. The hope for a better future is bleak, but there is still hope.

As long as we hold on believing in a future free of abject

poverty and senseless violence, there is still hope. Every single person in this room is here because they *believe* there is still hope, but our window is narrowing.

Already, our children are brought up to believe that this system is the best it ever can be. They are taught that the pain and suffering they live, day in and day out, is the only way that things can ever be. Our children, if you can believe it, are taught that the very people and things that take food out of their mouths and pollute the air they breathe are also the very things that are needed to make the world go round.

They are taught that the suffering they feel is for God and Country. As children watch the world wither and die around them, they are told there is no greater honor than to suffer it. *This* is the world in which we live and *this* is the very reason why everyone in this room continues to fight! The starving masses cannot imagine a world better than their own, but everyone in this room can.

Not only can we imagine it, we can make it so! This world of poverty, pollution, suffering, and war is not a world that we who have assembled here believe in, nor is it a world that we can accept. It is a world where each day a new child suffers the agonies of our age. This cannot continue to be. It is what the world is at this moment, but we *have* to firmly believe that this must not continue to be.

61

Our beliefs, our *convictions,* can very well make the difference we want to see in the world. Every single soul in this room is here because we refuse to live in a world plagued by war, poverty, pollution, and corruption. We *believe* in a future where the common man and common woman have enough to eat and a place to sleep. We *believe* that this world of greed can and *will* be destroyed. Destroyed so that a new world, like the phoenix from ashes, can right the wrongs of this decrepit world that leaves so many behind.

We are here not only for our own children, but for every child that is born into poverty and despair. A world ruined by the ills of our age is no world for our children. As long as death and profit are one in the same, we will not rest. It is important now, more than ever, that people of our good conscience need to stand against the ailing wrongs of society.

I ask all of you. Though you have already done so much, that you double down and do more. I ask you to help us help '*the people*' and bring this fight to the halls of legislation. We do not fight with the force which we oppose. A violent war is not a war that we will win, it is solidarity of thought that wins out in the end. I, and other members of our proud organization, will meet in a week with the leaders of this ailing nation. While we meet, as many people as possible need to rally.

The souls who have been touched by our great organization

and our fellows in thought will rally in peaceful solidarity against the degradation of this world steeped in greed and corruption. In this world which makes so many suffer through the pains of war and starvation, a line must be drawn. The people must rise, and the people desecrated by war and poverty must be a part of it. We have fought, but it is not just *our* fight to be won. The fight needs to be won by those who suffer the most.

I ask you, each and every one of you, to suffer as best as you can with *the people, the people* to whom we owe our service. As we approach a historic meeting with the leaders of this once great nation, I ask you to support our effort by whatever means aside from violence. It heartens my heart to see you all here, but I beg that you go one step further. Rally as many people as you can to march for freedom of thought and a better world.

We do not need a violent revolution, we need a revolution of thought, we need a revolution of solidarity.

I thank you all for your continued support. Raise a glass, 'to the fight for a world free of poverty, free of war, and free of greed. *To the future!*'"

Richard trailed off and went silent, caught up in his own memory. He remembered how the entire room full of people in tailored suits and beautiful dresses had taken to their feet cheering for his father. Several of the men who had spoken before rushed to Richard's father's side to wring his hand. It was nearly a full minute before the crowd settled back into their seats. Richard's mother, for the first time in the evening, was truly caught up by the excitement and beamed in the direction of his father. That moment was the last time Richard could really remember seeing the pure and unburdened stars in her eyes.

Richard downed the rest of his beer. The world had started its familiar spinning. At some point during his story a few of the old-timers in the bar had leaned in to hear his recollection of his father's speech. Even the barkeep had wandered over to hear what Richard had to say.

There was a sort of breathless vacuum that followed his last words. Several of the old-timers looked eager to hear more, but Richard just casually tapped his glass on the counter wanting a refill. Mark had a look of reverence for his friend plastered on his face. After a few seconds the barkeep shuffled over to refill Richard's glass, looking tentatively at Richard as if he wanted Richard to continue the story.

Richard had said as much as he could remember, so he just pushed his glass to the edge of the bar. Staring directly ahead, he sat silently waiting for his refill.

No one would have guessed, and Richard certainly didn't show it, but the thought of seeing his mother beaming that one last time had brought a lump into his throat and tears to the back of his eyes. Though he was able to project a look of calm reserve, he was in fact on the verge of choking up over the images racing through his head.

Finally, one of the other patrons in the bar cleared his throat and asked, "What happened with the rally?"

At first, Richard looked as if he hadn't heard the question and sat staring intently at his now full glass. The patron who asked caught Mark's eye and Mark just shrugged. Mark knew Richard. Bouts of silence were commonplace in their relationship. Mark had, over time, just come to accept that Richard's moody demeanor was the result of some of the strange things that he talked about. By Mark's calculations, it must just come with the territory of having a mind like Richard's.

The patron that had asked turned away from Richard, clearly giving up on hearing more of the story. Richard collected his thoughts and turned to answer:

"I don't know," Richard said audibly. "Truth be told, I don't actually know."

The people in the bar turned expectantly. Even the bartender who had retreated beyond earshot, came sauntering back. They waited a few moments before Richard got the rest of his thought out.

"I was never really told what happened. All I can remember was about a week later some guy rang our doorbell and came in to tell my mother that my father wasn't coming back. Other than a small, stifled sob from her and a few mutterings of the man, the only thing I heard was that he wasn't going to be coming back. My mother brought me into my room, shut the door, and went back out to talk to the man. I don't even know who the man was, my mother never did tell me." He trailed off, turned forward, and returned his attention to his beer.

After a few seconds he shook his whiskey glass and pointed at Mark's to be filled. The patron told Richard that he was sorry to hear that. Richard looked down the bar and could tell that people felt pity for him, which was nice of them, but not as nice as the whiskey and beer that sat in front of him.

Chapter 10

They found themselves stumbling back through the industrial district, about to go into the rundown one. Richard could tell that Mark was apprehensive at the thought of having to cross back through the squalor that stood between them and their dormitory. Richard was fairly drunk, so he was even more dismissive of Mark's fears than when they had crossed it the first time.

It had already been late when they first crossed the decrepit landscape, but several hours had passed. Though Mark had never seen it firsthand, it was common knowledge that rampant gangs wandered the poorest districts vandalizing out of boredom and mugging or looting anything of remote value. Worse still were the "Citizen Watchers."

For as long as Richard could remember, police had maintained a fairly reclusive presence and were reluctantly used. The police, as an organization, tried to maintain the image of actually upholding laws. Richard had heard his father explain that they had been used more widely, both for law enforcement as well as a means of control, years ago–but that brutality scandal after brutality scandal had forced them to change the way they operated.

Most of the police officers Richard had ever seen were obviously well fed, whereas Citizen Watchers were barely distinguishable from the starving citizens they so often harassed. The neat uniforms and fancy equipment of formal police were comically fancy when compared to the haphazard vests and crude blunt weapons used by The Citizens Watch. No public records were available on the city's expenditures, but it was easy to see that the city had fully embraced The Citizens Watch as the inexpensive and convenient solution to public solidarity that they were.

Richard had already started middle management school when The Citizens Watch had been created, so he must have been at least 18. But right around that time, the city appointed the first round of the violent pseudo cops to be unleashed on the city. City officials were all over the news (which at the time was already mostly just pamphlets and billboards posted all over the city, because shockingly few people had reliable radios let alone a working computer that had even somewhat consistent internet or a television that could be connected) and talked about how the program would put more eyes on the streets in order to deter looters, vandals, and all manner of other criminals.

What they were really releasing, and they knew damn well they were doing it, was a blight of criminals with immunity from the law in order to scare people off of the streets. The Citizen Watchers were never intended to deal with the vandals or looters. They were intended, and instructed, to scare the everyday run-of-the-mill impoverished people from assembling in any numbers on the street. This was in response to the starving protesting mobs that had erupted.

He remembered those days. Back then Richard cared more and drank less, he even went to a few of the rallies. Unlike the room full of elegantly dressed people listening to his father's impassioned speech, the rallies were extremely disorganized mobs of starving people being yelled directions at by moderately intelligible leaders. Richard, being one of the few slightly educated people in attendance, caught every last broken sentence and misused word. Eventually his frustration with the organizers outweighed his frustration with the world, so he stopped going to rallies.

He stopped at just the right time. Shortly after the last rally he went to, the army was called in to put down all protesters. After one bid for the crowds to disperse, the soldiers took aim and fired until every protester either lay dead on the ground or had scattered out of sight. The few timid protests that rose up afterwards were quickly disbanded by the newly appointed Citizen Watchers. The Citizen Watchers had such great success at instilling fear into the hearts of the poor and downtrodden that even after months of no protesting, the city doubled and then tripled the number of Citizen Watchers they unleashed on the city.

Richard had, unknown to Mark, come across both looters and Citizen Watchers in some of his drunken night wanderings. He had figured out that a certain drunken demeanor mixed with a sarcastically portrayed naive alien curiosity amused the vandals who were, in fact, just out looking for fun in the first place. Citizen Watchers were not that simple. The one-time Richard had made the mistake to wander by three Citizen Watchers in the middle of the night he had come off worse for it.

They surrounded him like hungry jackals. In illiterate "Who's you, boy" type of speech, they asked nearly unintelligible circular questions while shoving him between each other like a pinball. After a few moments they got bored with his lack of response and one of them landed a hooked punch right in his gut knocking the wind out of him. As he keeled over another one sucker punched him square in the right ear. Richard's ears began to ring and his vision became blurred.

The only sound he could hear over the ringing was their

idiotic laughing. He was thrown to the ground and kicked in the stomach. For a moment it seemed like they had had their fun, but for good measure he was picked up by the hair as a fist slammed into his cheekbone which laid him out on the ground leaving the whole world spinning painfully just beyond his half-closed eyes. Each of them took one final kick at his crumpled body and moved on into the night looking for their next prey.

The buildings of the sooty industrial district gave way to the rundown decrepit buildings of the slums. Mark was nearly beside himself with anxiety. Mark's eyes flitted in every direction at once waiting to see the shadows that he imagined would give way to violent men.

Richard was calm. He had been through districts like this enough times to know where to look for possible marauding Citizen Watchers and which side streets to duck down if he should happen to see some. After all, running away from Citizen Watchers fed their power-hungry egos without them having to tenderize a person's body. He had imparted nothing of his experiences to Mark, but he appreciated Mark was bothered by the apparent decay, poverty, and squalor.

Richard had often mused over the idea of what would happen if the shit brains in his dorm and in his classes ever ended up marooned in the middle of a squalor-filled district. He imagined the fear on their faces mixed with their imparted societal disdain of abject poverty. The thought of their hatred of the so-labeled *unproductive poor* giving way to the terror of a world in which so many lived brought him a feeling of righteous justice.

He imagined the feeling they would have of shattered security as they were faced with the product of their dutiful devotion to a corrupt system. Janis would be the best. Every time he imagined her self-righteous bitchy face turning to horror made him feel better about the fact that one day *she* would label *him* as 'unproductive.'

She was on the fast track to being a beautiful cog in the machine that made this horrendously unjust world a reality. The blame for every person who died of pneumonia, every person who was beaten to death by gangs or Citizen Watchers, every person who wasted away out of starvation, every family that lost a member to prison for stealing to get by, and most of all for every child that suffered and died–abandoned by their impoverished parents would be laid directly on her feet. Richard might be 'unproductive,' but at least he would never be responsible for so much pain and suffering.

They heard a racket a few blocks away. A woman sobbing rang out against the night, reverberating back and forth between the crumbling buildings of the street. Both Richard and Mark stopped dead in their tracks. Mark had a look of terror stretched across his paralyzed face, frozen and not breathing. Richard looked around intently to see where the sound had come from. Breaks in the sobbing revealed men's voices and laughter. The memory of his violent encounter with the Citizen Watchers flashed through the forefront of his mind.

First Richard felt fear, but it gave way to anger. A vision of somebody undergoing the same humiliating encounter that once happened to him caused him to clench his fist. Mark, still not having uttered a breath, turned to his friend and was alarmed because he could tell Richard was about to do something that could get him killed. Richard began to literally shake with anger and his previous drunken posturing was replaced with furious concentration. He unclenched his right fist and reached into his coat pocket for a cigarette. Bringing it up to his mouth he unclenched his left fist and dug for a lighter. To Mark, this unexpected reaction was too much.

"What are you doing?" he hysterically whispered.

Richard didn't reply. He didn't even glance in Mark's direction. His body showed that he had resigned himself to the notion of doing *something* to intervene. The sobs grew louder as Richard began to walk towards the scene. Mark stood petrified watching what he imagined was his friend walking towards suicide. Some small force in Mark tried to stir up a shred of courage in order to follow his friend, but the terror kept him rooted in place. Mark danced back and forth from one foot to the other, completely overcome with fear.

What Mark thought or felt was the last thing on Richard's mind. All he could bring himself to think about was that some woman in the dead of night was being harassed by a couple of shit brained violent pricks. Every muscle of his wiry body was tensed and ready to pounce, anger coursed through every vein. They will pay, he thought. They will pay for what they did to me, what they are doing to her, and what they have done to every single miserable person they have ever come across. He knew, obviously, that these Citizen Watchers were not the same ones who accosted him, but they would pay, nonetheless.

The thought of Janis ran through his mind again. He mustered every feeling of disgust for her and her fucking obedience into a solidified resolve that somebody would finally pay and that he would the one to make them. He wished she could see how productive he was about to be.

As he rounded the corner he saw two men, one was thin and about his height while the other was a short pudgy fellow who was snorting like a pig in laughter at the woman that lay on the ground before him. He stopped for a moment to watch, collecting his nerves.

Richard was not without fear. Mark might have been right that crossing Citizen Watchers was akin to suicide. If their cries drew more of their ranks he was almost guaranteed to be arrested or worse. He watched as the thin one kicked soot into the sobbing woman's face which caused the fat one to double up his laughter. The laughter of his fatass dragoon comrade was obviously spurring the thin one on. He reached down and grabbed the woman by her hair and spit in her face. Richard was enraged beyond any amount of fear and started forward, but stopped short. A blurry shadow seemingly dropped out of the night crashing into the thin Watcher.

Richard could hardly believe what he was seeing. The thin one pitched violently forward and there was a loud crunch as his head smashed into the decaying brick wall in front of him. Before his body had even crumpled to the ground, the shadow wheeled around and landed a full force kick into the piggy one's groin. The snorting laughter of just moments before was replaced with a high-pitched nasal cry.

The fatass sobbed like a child, grabbing at his newly collapsed testicles. Richard stood in disbelief, stifling a laugh. Not in a million years would he have imagined that some shadowy figure would drop out of the sky and deliver the justice he had only moments before decided to be an agent of. He watched as the shadow grabbed a nearby discarded glass bottle and brought it down squarely on top of the piggy's head. True to form, he squealed as he too crumpled to the ground. The sobbing woman was in shock. Only moments before she had been in a hellish nightmare and the turn of events seemed too good to be true. As the shadow turned to the woman and spoke, Richard went into shock.

There was no mistaking that voice. It was the voice of the beautiful girl who had whispered something about Citizen Watchers and then helped him to get home when he wanted to sleep in the alleyway. It was the voice of the girl who had his mother's starry eyes. She helped the woman to her feet, gave both men one last kick in the stomach, ushered the woman out of the alley and out of sight.

As Richard walked back to his friend his mind was a blur. Just seeing the girl from the alley reminded him of his stinging shoulders when she crashed down on him, but the thing that he remembered most were the stars in her eyes.

In silent disbelief, Richard approached his terrified friend. Mark, not having seen the events, looked at Richard as if he was the cause of all of the commotion. Mark's look was that of disbelieving reverence. Richard said nothing to Mark about what had transpired.

Chapter 11

It was already afternoon when Richard woke from a restless sleep, the memory of the beautiful girl's starry eyes was the first thought that flashed through his mind.

A boom of thunder rattled the walls. Lightning storms were a fairly common thing, but rarely did thunder sound so close to his dorm. He slid off his aged blanket, swung himself to his feet (so that the blood could rush from his head), and stumbled forward to his desk.

His raspy cough hit him in a wave. He nearly doubled over, clutching the desk to support himself. Amidst the coughing he reached into his desk drawer for a cigarette. At first his hand only brushed past the rosewood handle of his father's revolver, but he doubled it back to clench firmly on the grip.

For the first time in years, he brought the weapon out of the desk drawer. He pointed the barrel at the window as a flash of lightning struck a building visible directly across from his dorm. The walls shook furiously. He only had two boxes of ammunition, but at least he had something.

Dark rain was pouring outside, the kind that seared the grounds. Richard placed the pistol back in its drawer and shuffled a cigarette out of its package. Stifling a cough, he grabbed a match and lit it. The smoke in his lungs chased away the surge of anger that had brought him to raise the revolver out of its drawer. He calmly slunk into the chair in front of his desk and flipped the switch on his battery powered radio, which rested, half buried, by papers on the corner of his desk. A harsh tone sounded several times before a monotone voice began its report.

"This is a broadcast from the Central District Weather Bureau. In effect. Extreme lighting storm warning. City watershed has reached surface levels in many areas of the district. Travel is unadvised. Acidic rainfall levels exceed Central District health advisories. Limited exposure is advised. This advisory is in effect until future notice. This is a broadcast from the Central Weather Bureau..."

He flipped the radio off and dug another cigarette out of its package. He remembered always listening to music on his radio when he had first come to live in the dorm. Back then the power was actually still moderately reliable. Now that the power was out more often than not, he had to rely on batteries. He had to ration his use of them because batteries had become very difficult to come by and expensive as a result. Knowing there was no way he was going to bring himself to cross the grounds to his classes that day, he opened the bottom drawer of his desk and fished for a bottle of whiskey. The glass that sat towards the back of his desk, one of two in his room, had been used dozens of times; Richard rarely washed them–but he drank out of them anyway. He filled his glass half full of the cheap and bitter whiskey. As the liquor hit him, his mind flashed for a moment back to his childhood house.

He remembered the refrigerator which was divided down the middle with a freezer that contained ice trays. When he was younger there were rarely ever power outages and he could remember filling glasses with ice and the sweet juices his mother used to buy. The memories of the comfort and convenience of his childhood were in stark contrast to the world that he now found himself in.

After seeing the woman from the alleyway twice, thoughts of his mother also made him think of the starry-eyed girl from the alley who seemed to have the same passion that his mother had when he was younger.

The more Richard thought about it–the memories of such a girl, memories that were absolutely seared into his brain, in those run down and decrepit alleys seemed ridiculous. If he hadn't seen it he would never have believed it was possible. The alley he had contemplated passing out in where she came crashing down on *him* and the alley where he had approached the Citizen Watchers were miles apart and in two completely different districts. In a city of millions of people, it seemed absolutely impossible that he could run into the same girl in the same way that many miles apart.

Suddenly his mind jolted back to what he had half-heard her whisper. All he could remember was that she had said something about Citizen Watchers, but he was almost sure that she had given him some type of apology. The way she had come crashing into the thin Citizen Watcher was exactly the same as how she must have come crashing down into him, so it made sense if it was an apology.

He took a large gulp from his glass and choked at the bitterness.

The idea of such a girl was an insane thought, but he had seen it with his own eyes. Apparently, she was a girl that roamed the streets in the dead of night–looking to stop violent pseudo cops from harassing people in the city.

The idea that somebody could have stars in their eyes and

was actually doing something to help the poor and downtrodden was a new and alien concept. Richard had come to expect that everyone he ran into, at some level or other (other than Mark and maybe Old Dirge), was a pawn of the corrupt and polluted world around him–but she defied that notion.

His building shook at the foundation as a bolt of lightning struck the lightning pole on the roof.

Richard heard faint cries from doors down the hall. He filled his glass with more of the repugnant whiskey, got to his feet, and walked over to the window to look at the storm outside. Even though it was the middle of the day, thick dark clouds blocked out the sun giving the day the appearance of night.

A downpour of rain made it hard to see clearly in the distance, but from what he could see–bolts of lightning dotted the blurred skyline of the city. Soft waves of thunder rung out every few seconds punctuated by booms sounding from strikes to closer buildings. There had been plenty of lightning storms since he had lived in his dorm, but he could never remember a storm like this.

He watched a blinding light obscure the world outside his window as another bolt of lightning shook the building. There was nothing he could do but take another pull from his glass. He didn't know exactly how he knew, but he knew that the system was responsible for this too. They were responsible for everything in this run down and miserable fucking world.

He remembered storms when he was a child:

His father and mother would turn the lights off and they would sit and play cards by candlelight. On such occasions, his father would talk about how these storms were unnatural. He would say that people could help stop them from happening so frequently if they just tried to make a difference. Richard never exactly understood what his father was talking about, but his memory did always come back to those memories whenever there was a severe storm.

As he thought about it, his father had never really said that people made them in the sense that there was some type of an on and off switch. He claimed that there was something about the industrial districts that caused a change to the world and caused storms like the one that was now striking his building. His father never gave him the details about how that would work, which was one of the reasons he couldn't explain to someone else why the trees were dying.

When Richard was younger, he would ask his teachers if what his father said was true, but they would tell him to stop asking questions and change the subject. Even Richard's mother sometimes snapped at his father for just talking about it.

The most vivid recollection he had of her snapping on his

father was in the weeks before the man came to tell his mother that his father wouldn't be coming back. One day, in the middle of the summer, a snowstorm appeared out of nowhere and set in for days. The storm was the first of its kind that Richard could remember. His dad brooded around the house and would launch into diatribes about how a few greedy people were causing the ruin of the world. He would repeatedly say that it could all be stopped if people would just take action.

Finally his mother, who had already begun to show signs of the hollow look of her years to come, yelled at him to stop it. Richard was surprised and his father was positively shocked. In his earliest years, his mother had always worn a look of admiration when his father would talk about the world and how to change it. On that day, her admonishing look and tone were foreign to the house.

His father stood looking dumbfounded for a moment before rushing to sweep her into his arms in a loving embrace. She stifled a sob, but after a few moments her face gave way to warmth and the incident passed. In truth the incident only passed for a very short time, because her harsh tone and sunken look would mark her for the rest of her life.

Richard quit the window, walked back to his desk, sat down, and refilled his glass. The whiskey had begun to take effect. His head felt light and the sound of thunder became muffled. Richard dug another cigarette out of his desk and flipped the switch on his desk light. Nothing. Of course it was nothing. It was the biggest storm he could remember...and the power was cut. 'I suppose it might be the lightning,' Richard thought to himself in a less angry tone. He fished through his desk for a fresh candle, set it on top of his desk, and lit the wick with his cigarette.

There was a knock on his door. He was startled and shocked. Nobody ever came to his room other than Janice and that was only at night. Since it was the middle of the afternoon, it couldn't be her.

Back when Janice and Richard would still talk, she would remind him how unproductive he was and how if he didn't become more productive, he would end up a homeless drunk like Old Dirge. She would tell him how embarrassed she would be if somebody were to ever catch her near him, Janis was even quicker with judgment than she was at reciting bullshit slogans. She made him gag worse than the repugnant liquid he was forcing down his throat.

The knock came again, so Richard took to his feet and walked to the door to see who could possibly be knocking in the middle of the day. The knock came a third time before he opened the door to Mark's face.

Mark had an almost hysterical look about him and he was

biting his fingernails while shifting his weight back and forth over his feet. Richard stood in silence taking in the look of his clearly disheveled friend. Mark was the first one to break the awkward meeting.

"Um, hello Richard." He said sheepishly.

Already intoxicated, Richard was not able to guess the cause of Mark's apparent apprehension. Mark stood frozen, clearly wanting to say something but not being able to articulate it.

Even though he was already drunk, after a moment, it dawned on Richard. His anxiety-ridden friend had probably sat tossing and turning the whole night imagining what had happened in the alley from the night before.

Mark was overly skittish, so his imagination had created an all-out fight for life and death scene between Richard and the unknown Citizen Watchers.

"Why don't you come in?" asked Richard.

Mark entered the room and Richard gestured for Mark to pull up a chair sitting next to the window. He grabbed the second glass off of his desk, filled it almost to the brim with whiskey, and handed it to Mark. In the ensuing silence, Richard dug another cigarette out of its package and lit it. Mark nervously sipped some of the liquid from his glass, which caused him to gag slightly.

Mark cared a great deal more about what Richard thought of him than he cared about anybody else, especially considering his Gran was no longer with him. Richard was just staring blankly at the lightning storm outside of the window, so Mark allowed thoughts of his Gran to seep into his head while waiting for his friend to come around.

Mark wasn't much one for crying, but the fairly recent memory of her funeral came flooding back. He remembered the tears flowing down his face while the pastor of the church his Gran had often visited spoke to a nearly empty room. There were only two other people at the funeral, Mr. Moliere who worked the counter at the ration store where she got their food and Ms. Schuler who had worked at the same ration office as his grandma.

It wasn't the memory of her funeral that *really* tugged at his mind though, what was racing through his mind over and over was wondering what she would have thought if she would have known where he was last night and what (he thought) Richard had done. She had always emphasized how important it was to never cause a stir and never to get into trouble, but with Richard last night–he had nearly done just that.

Richard snapped out of his blank staring at the window. He knew that Mark was poor. He knew that Mark was poor because Mark was thin. Granted, after having access to the school rations program Mark had taken on a healthier look, but it was easy to notice that he was short and underdeveloped from a long hard life of abject poverty and hunger.

Richard was aware that many of his middle management peers came from wealthy or well-to-do families. They came from families with more than enough in life to afford to spend as much as they wanted on the sweet and fatty foods sold at commissaries. Families that could afford to buy decent clothes and plenty of useless trinkets. Most of the fatass dragoons had never once thought what life might be like for people like Mark and his grandmother, working endlessly in miserable conditions for just enough ration credits to allow them not to completely starve to death.

No, Richard thought, most of his so-called "*peers*" had grown up in mindlessly comfortable families where they were taught the bullshit slogans reinforced by this miserable school. They were taught that the reason people like Mark's grandma had to work until they dropped dead from whatever illness their harsh lives finally dealt them was that they were lazy *unproductive*. As if the working poor had somehow committed some worldly offense that justly condemned them to a life of misery, poverty, and fruitless labor.

The disillusionment of his "*peers*" was so thoroughly ingrained in them that even as grown children, because to call them adults would be a rather drastic misrepresentation, they already looked at Mark as part of the *unproductive* and undeserving poor.

The thought that these fatass dragoons saw Mark as a categorically subhuman person made Richard furious. On numerous occasions, much to his shame, he had watched as members of *The Productivity Club* and members of (what Richard considered to be) pointless athletic teams corner Mark and harass him about the clothes he was wearing and anything else they could come up with.

The whiskey made his head swim away from thoughts of the fatass dragoons and he turned his attention to his mousey and frightened friend sitting in front of him. He couldn't help but let out a small laugh at the scared look on Mark's face, which caused Mark to squirm in his chair. It might have been the whiskey, and it might have been Richard wanting a break on a dark dismal day, or possibly both, but he decided to have a little fun at his gullible friend's expense. His drunken head concocted a story of how he bravely faced down Citizen Watchers.

Mark finally broke the silence:

"Um, Richard. About last night..."

Richard played into the cue, "Right, last night. It was certainly something. I can hardly believe it (which was actually true) ...that poor old woman. I don't feel the least bit sorry about what I did to those bastards. Even Citizen Watchers can't treat such an innocent and defenseless person like that on my watch. I couldn't help but teach them a lesson on civility."

Mark's face was an image of pure terror. "But they are Citizen Watchers!" he interceded hysterically.

"All the better for them to be taught a lesson. Those bastards need it and then some! I would be positively disappointed if I didn't think I'd cracked one of their heads wide open!" The look on Mark's face was so amusing that Richard couldn't help but go further, "I would be even more disappointed if I wasn't certain that one of them is still laying limp in the alley!" "Richard!" was all the response that the terrified Mark could muster.

"The other one didn't fare much better. I got one straight in the eye and tore the other's arm right out of its socket, but what was I supposed to do?" he shot rhetorically at Mark.

"But, but, but..."

"I couldn't possibly have stood by and waited while thugs harassed a poor innocent woman! There is nothing more to it," he said with finality.

Mark sat, eyes popping out of his head, trying to imagine how the horrific scene might have played out. His speechlessness gave way to nervous rocking. Richard took two huge gulps and finished his glass.

"I am tired of whiskey. That leaves rum or vodka, any

preference?" he asked nonchalantly.

Mark lost it, "How can you be thinking about whiskey! You might have killed somebody! Richard, this is serious...If you get caught!"

Having had enough fun at his little game he looked straight at his mousey friend and laughed a good-spirited laugh. Mark looked puzzled.

"I didn't actually do any of that."

"But...but..." Mark stammered. His face blushed a deep red as he realized that his friend had been playing at his gullibility.

"Listen to this, because what actually happened is far less plausible than what I just told you. When I got into the alley, a girl fell out of the sky and crashed into one of the Watchers. It sounds insane, I know..." he trailed off for a moment before proceeding to tell Mark the entirety of the story from when she had landed on him in a completely different alley all the way to when he watched her run off down the alley with the woman she had just saved and disappeared out of sight.

Chapter 12

She stood crouched in the shadow of a steam vent on top of the '*raven's nest*,' the name she had given to the five-story building she was perched on. It had easy routes down to the street in multiple directions.

She listened for any noise. Sometimes, when all was quiet, she heard the moans of the cold and hungry; other times she heard drunken men stumbling down the streets and sometimes she would hear the racket made by the Citizen Watchers.

Her dad would die of shock if he ever found out that she snuck out of the manor by night to tussle with the violent psychos who terrorized the city. Her brother, who had *absolutely* no room to talk, would be furious. Her brother had always insisted on treating her like she was his baby sister. He was actually a year and a half younger than she was, so she hoped he would eventually get over it. Even if she wasn't his baby sister, he wouldn't be able to see past her being his sister. She didn't care what they would think, she knew that what she was doing was right.

She always brought along money whenever she went out on her nighttime adventures. Whenever she would hear the moaning suffering of the hungry, she would make her way down from her perch and give whomever enough money for a few days of food.

She felt bad that she couldn't do more for them, but she took pride that she was doing *something*. Most people did nothing. The frequenters of her father's gatherings sometimes talked idly in passing about the rapidly crumbling buildings around the city and the terrible poverty of the people living in them. None of them seemed aware that every morning teams of the DDEH (Department of Disposal of Expired Humans) combed alleys to clear out those who died of poisoned water, lack of food, and hypothermia. The existence of poverty was an inconvenient thought for them and despite claiming to be compassionate and being seemingly rational people, they all had a way of turning on a sort of delusional thinking. Most of them seemed convinced that somebody was going to do something about it, but then they also supported the Citizen Watchers violently terrorizing desperate and vulnerable people.

The crackdown where the military had been used was the final straw for her brother. He woke her up in the middle of the night to tell her about an indiscriminate shooting of a crowd of protesters. Once her grogginess had worn off, she was as mortified as he looked. When her brother first started talking loudly to his father and guests about how the ever-increasing military presence in the streets was going to lead to the destruction of everything; her brother had seemed strange, hostile, and erratic.

She did not understand him at first. A large part of that was because her brother had not come up with a very good way of explaining himself at that point. As the horror of what had been done to a group of protesters sank in, she knew that he had been right all along.

Her first worry had been that their father was involved. Her brother had assured her that he wasn't, but her brother was still furious. In her brother's mind, their father was every part as guilty as whatever other general had passed along the orders. "Doing nothing to stop it was as bad as doing it," her brother had said.

She still had never been able to hold a grudge against her father. She knew that her father could be sympathetic and sometimes thought her brother unfairly judged him. But as the world got worse and worse she could sense that her father's sympathies had dwindled and often thought more and more about running off to stay with her brother. Her brother was right;

something had to be done. Even if it was small, it still *had* to be something.

She was certainly not a person who was doing nothing. The nights she spent in her raven's nest had helped dozens and dozens of people. If she had to defend herself to her brother, she knew her brother would quickly retort, "Sure it saves dozens, but we are talking about millions. It's too risky!" It *was* risky, but it was something. To those dozens of people, it was everything. Sometimes her nighttime ventures wore her out for days afterward, but she always knew they were worth it. Plus, it was exciting for her.

Most of her life, she had been raised to fit into the fairly lackluster world around her. A world in which everybody seemed to be deliberate and structured. None of them would ever understand the rush of being out alone at night. Most of them wouldn't understand it out of cowardice. She, like her father and brother, was brave. It annoyed her that they would get angry at her for putting herself in the same kinds of danger they both had many times themselves.

From what she understood, her father had been a war hero once. Sometimes when he would drink, he would rub his left ribs or bend down and rub his right thigh before launching into stories of the days of his youthful fighting camaraderie. He would show her the scars from his bullet wounds. It wasn't just the medals on the military suits he wore that made his stories true, he had the scars to prove it. When he would tell his battle stories to the people at his parties, many also wearing military decorations, the looks on their faces were that of complete belief. However, unlike her father, she was pretty sure none of them had taken two bullets in the heat of battle. She also believed him because he was an honest man. Even her brother had admiration for their father's adamant belief that a man must be able to be taken at his word.

It had been eerily silent all night, which saddened her. She knew that the poisonous sludge which had been falling from the skies had ended many hungry cries for the last time. She was glad that she hadn't been able to make it out for over a week after the worst of the storm had passed because it always tore her up inside to watch DDEH vehicles combing the streets after a bad storm. It was terrible because of how often they would stop. Sometimes she could hear the workers complain about having to wrestle a body into an almost entirely full van.

Something stirred a few blocks over.

She could hear a set of voices carry over the building tops and her nerves kicked in. The rush of possible danger was the feeling she loved most about her night walking, fear and excitement mortally intertwined. She wondered if the feeling was the same as what her father felt before his battles so many years ago. Her brother, though no stranger to battles himself, most likely had never felt it because he was always stubbornly strong and unafraid. She could hear her brother saying to her, "What is there to fear? Death is probably better than this shithole of a world and living can be very overrated." The lackadaisical way he would say things like that always unsettled her. She knew he wasn't exactly looking to die, but his mentality made him reckless, and she was scared to lose him.

The voices were clearer now. Over the quiet of the night, she could hear laughter and unmistakably drunken banter. It didn't sound much like Citizen Watchers, the voices were too friendly and the conversation was silly and unintelligible. Still, she figured, nothing had happened all night so she might as well go have a look.

As she climbed down, the memory of the last time she was out flashed into her mind. She had gone quite a bit out of her way to explore a new district. The memories of the completely decrepit buildings and the mass of people huddled in alleys were still fresh. It was the only night she had ever given out all of her money. She had also won quite the scuffle against two Citizen Watchers who were harassing a homeless woman. Her brother wouldn't get it, but she was actually helping people–which, at this point, was more than their father could say.

There was an unexplainable queerness to the memory of that night. Shortly after she had landed a swift kick to one of their miserable sets of testicles, as she had turned to dash away, she thought she had seen a shadow at the mouth of the alley watching her. She had told herself later that it was just a trick of light, but it didn't do anything to help her forget how the hair had raised on the back of her neck. Her hair hadn't exactly been raised out of fear, it had felt similar to the night she mistook the drunken young man for a Watcher.

She didn't know why it had been so unsettling to her. It may partially have been that she worried about the wrong judgment she had made when she crashed into the innocent young man. If the young man hadn't braced himself as she tackled him to the concrete, he might very well have been badly injured. On more than one occasion, she was pretty sure that she had given a few of the Citizen Watchers lasting wounds.

The night she landed on the young man was an extremely vivid memory. It wasn't just her regret at having attacked someone who was not a Citizen Watcher that made the memory vivid, it was the pair of eyes that turned to look at her after the young man had picked himself up off of the ground:

In the faint light of a streetlamp, his eyes had flashed steel gray and pierced right through hers. With the heavily drunken way he tried to orient himself, she could hardly believe that he would be capable of focusing on anything, let alone focus long enough to curiously stare right through her. She was very familiar with interesting reactions from men after they realized who they were being terrorized by, but his reaction was different. He had appeared curious rather than angry at having been knocked down and stood silently once he had gotten himself off the ground. His brow had lifted as his cheeks and face warmed up to the sight of a strange girl in an alley.

Even though the young man had been a drunken mess, she had still taken note that he was rather handsome. Not handsome like the clean-cut buttoned-down boys that had been paraded in front of her nonstop, but handsome precisely because he was not like the clean or buttoned-down boys that had been paraded in front of her. It had obviously been a while since he had shaved and he smelled strongly of tobacco smoke and beer, but behind the beard was a stoic jawline and high cheekbones. Conspicuously perfect eyebrows framed what she now saw to be blue-green, yet somehow also gray, eyes. Thick, messy hair topped his pronounced forehead.

Strangely, his eyes hadn't wavered from her face. She couldn't remember any boy in years who resisted the urge to ogle at her breasts the second they saw her. It didn't seem to be a thought for him. He was fixated on just looking into her eyes. His unadulterated gaze had brought a blush to her cheeks which had caused her to turn away.

She had realized that he wasn't going to make it far with as drunk as he was and asked him where he was going. All he could get out were a few drunken words and just pointed in a direction. She took pity and wrapped her arm around him to help him to get home. As he clumsily threw his arm around her back, his hand lightly brushed her breast before coming to rest around her navel. It had caused her heart to skip for a second. It wasn't as though she had never been intimate with a boy, but something about the drunken mess she began to help stagger down the street felt different. Even the memory still made the hair on the back of her neck bristle.

She pushed the memory aside because she had made it down to a short building right above where the two voices were going to be walking. It was always entertaining whenever she watched people roam the dark streets of the city. Whether it was Citizen Watchers or just drunk people, it never ceased to be interesting. When the two got close enough that she could make out who they were, the hair on her neck stood completely on end as the young man she had crashed into in the alley walked down the street. He was animatedly talking to a smaller boy that appeared a few years younger. It was so surreal that she decided to quit the night altogether and return to her father's manor hours before she would on a normal night of night wanderings.

Chapter 13

Richard looked up at the sky on his way to class. The lightning storm that had hit so hard had somehow given way to even darker clouds. The kind of clouds that he knew could easily dump the tar-like rain which eventually rotted buildings. Despite having seen the lightning storm, these clouds seemed darker and more pestilent than ever before.

It began to rain.

The sludge that fell to the ground smelled of gaseous chemicals. Richard was sure that this type of rain had all but killed the plants and trees the school had all over the grounds. What was worse, the power had been down for nearly a week. The school would turn on generators for the dorms twice a day for about an hour so students could shower and use the restroom and they ran them in the other buildings during classes. Other than that, not a single light anywhere in his dorm would even flicker. He could remember several times where the power had cut out for a day or two, which at the time had seemed like forever. The lack of power was causing everyone at his college, including himself, to start to worry.

For the last few days-every time he walked from his dorm to one of the lecture buildings, there was a fear (now bordering on hysteria) clearly visible on the empty round faces of the people around him. It would have amused him more if he wasn't stuck in the same hellhole. The nails on a chalkboard feeling he got whenever he heard their shit brain laughter had nowhere near the effect on him as the pitiful moans that rose from nearly every room every night.

On the bright side it had kept Janis away, which had actually reduced his frustration. While the power being out for such a lengthy stretch was certainly worry some-Richard was making do. He spent most of his free time at the bar (which had electricity produced by a pair of old beat-up generators) so the inconvenience, for him, wasn't all that bad. Sitting in his dark dorm with no power and too much time even had him resorting to attending most of his classes.

Spending more time actually sitting through the middle management classes he had come to loathe had him regularly thinking back to the upper-level middle management classes he took when he first came to the school. Back then, he remembered combing over statistics and learning the parts of the system that he would be in charge of (which would have included the rank-and-file middle management people like Janice). He had scraped by in most of his early classes–mainly by outscoring the bulk of his classmates on tests, until he was told that he had to stop and take the required beginner classes before being allowed to continue. Having to take the introduction classes sapped his motivation and it had been a five-year fight ever since.

For every somewhat interesting thing one of the teacher assistants said, there were easily a dozen insufferable things–especially in *understanding language.* He might have had a shot at one point to put his head down and squeak by some of the basics, but two days into 'understanding language' and he was up in arms.

As a chronic reader most of his life, he felt as if an entire language was trapped in his head. Every time he spoke before thinking about who he was talking to, there was a good chance the person would look at him like he was speaking a foreign language. The idiocy of it tore at him.

He thought in English as it was written by the authors of the books he had taken from his father's library. He spoke the English he had heard as a child. The type of English that he spoke was the same type that he had heard from the ghosts of the vibrant people who spoke so eloquently who came into and out of his parents' lives. He literally spoke the same language (both were English) as the people around him, but for some reason, people told him that he was strange and would be better off if he learned how to use the broken version that had come to dominate his world.

Almost a decade had gone by since his father disappeared, but the way Richard thought and spoke had not changed. He had no intention of changing either.

As he went to open the door to the building his classroom was in, he caught sight of his clothes in the reflection of the glass. It was his 'nice' coat, yet stains from the toxic rain had turned even that coat from light brown to black. Even his best coat smelled of the chemicals that the rain brought down.

The dim lights of the dorm that the generators were only powering a few precious hours a day were in stark contrast to the lights of the buildings full of classrooms. The lights in the building were as artificial and harsh as ever. He wondered how a school could justify not having more generators where people slept when it could get cold at nearly any time of year, yet made sure they could keep the harsh and artificial lights of lecture buildings going throughout the entire day. It seemed like not freezing to death should be more important than learning slogans, but in this rotten world that obviously wasn't going to be the case.

He would have even accepted if there was just a single generator to light the bathrooms at all times, which usually sat completely dark at night if the power was shut off.

He stopped just short of the door to his class and let out a deep exacerbated sigh in preparation of the frustration he was about to endure. It killed him to sit and watch people memorize the minimum amount of information before discarding it at their earliest convenience. Janis excelled at slogans for the duration of the classes, but she couldn't produce even half of them even weeks after she had taken them.

He glanced to the front of the class and saw '*positivity places*' scrolled on the board. Great, he thought–a minute into class and he was already pissed. He would have to sit and listen to a half hour of the horny dragoon who was the teacher's assistant teaching '*positivity places*' while trying to make his best attempts to smooth talk the giddily excitable beginner class girls.

It disturbed Richard that somebody who couldn't be a day younger than twenty-three would attempt obvious sexual advancements on barely of age girls who could (only through a technicality) be considered adults in front of a room full of people. He was the same age as most of the teacher's assistants and these girls seemed like children to him. What was more disturbing was how receptive some of them were to it. It wasn't as if it didn't make sense to Richard from a logical standpoint. The world was falling apart faster and faster, so the further and faster you could climb the better you would be. The world would come for them eventually too though, because nobody at the top of the ladder was ever going to give up their spots. Just another failing part of a terrible system.

The monologue in his head had caused him to miss the explanation the dragoon had made about what he wanted to hear back from the lime green sheet of paper that had been passed to him. When Richard was younger, schools gave kids books to go along with what they were saying, now they just gave a single piece of paper with a large font.

When to ask your manager: part 4.

- Have you tried positive words?
- Have you tried to smile?
- Have you tried telling them to read their employee booklet?
- Ask your manager.

Nearly every piece of paper had the same final step. There wasn't a single one in any class, middle management or upper middle management, that ever ended in; "figure out the solution to the problem."

It really wasn't their fault they were that way. He would be the same if he hadn't read so many books. Many of the other students even seemed smart when they were memorizing for what now passed for finals in this 'school'. Something happened right afterwards though–all the focus and thought seemed to melt away. They would immediately forget what they had learned. The other students would devolve into idle gossip and then pathetic boys would try to, as Old Dirge always said, "get their dick wet."

There was yelling in the hallway. The distraction was all the excuse Richard needed to get up and leave the class. He crumpled the useless green paper into a ball and threw it into the trash before stepping into the hallway to look around for the commotion. Richard immediately spotted Mark.

Chapter 14

As Mark trekked through the dark rain to class, he felt the all too familiar pains of a hangover. It was the same exhausting day that the days had been for the last week. Unlike Richard, he could hardly sleep at night even when he was drunk. He never got as drunk as Richard, so he thought it might be that he wasn't drunk enough. The problem was that Mark always threw up whenever he tried to keep up with his friend. He knew that Old Dirge had fun drinking. Richard was drunk and probably wouldn't remember it, but he summed up Old Dirge in a sentence one time; "The old fuck would probably be dead if it wasn't for the serenity he finds in alcohol." Richard was frequently able to make insightful observations.

He wished Richard didn't swear so much. It was funny enough when he was calling Old Dirge 'the old fuck,' but sometimes it got so bad when Richard drank that Mark wasn't sure Richard even knew what he was saying. Richard was a bit like Old Dirge. Richard knew a lot about things and it kept Mark entertained, but when the alcohol finally caught up to them–both changed. He enjoyed how Richard talked normally. He even liked how Richard used words he didn't know, but after too many (what were now Mark's favorite) whiskey sippers, it seemed like the only things Richard could say was fuck and shitbrain.

However, Old Dirge and Richard were also different. When Old Dirge got drunk, he became silly; when Richard got drunk, he would start to brood and shut down. Even though Richard was full of angst, at least he wasn't mean to Mark.

Mark had a way of always staying positive when people were mean to him. He had always been small. Both short and thin, he had always been the target of harassment by people bigger than him. He had always wondered what was fun for them about shoving around a scrawny kid.

Mark never said anything mean, he kept to himself, and always tried to wear a friendly smile, but for some reason–that made him stand out. Standing out was always something Mark tried to avoid, but he couldn't shake his friendly demeanor.

Richard's cynical observations had rubbed off on him a bit. He knew people picked on him more out of their own insecurities than his own. Still, Mark thought, it would be nice if people would just leave him alone.

For all Richard's alcoholism, cynicism, and erratic behavior-Richard was actually a really good friend. Richard treated Mark like a valid person and was patient with Mark whenever he explained any of the things that Richard liked to explain. Even when Richard would go into a frustrated fit, he never snapped and said anything mean about Mark.

Sometimes, especially after talking about Janis, he would turn sentimental towards Mark. He could hear Richard's drunken voice telling him, "You know why I like you, Mark? Because you're not a spoiled, good for nothing, fatass, idiot. Your Gran raised you right and I'm glad we are friends."

Mark would always twinge when his Gran was mentioned. He was glad he told Richard about her even if Richard was somewhat tactlessly unaware that it was a very sensitive subject with him. It bothered him at first when Richard would talk about her like she was still alive and waiting at home, but Mark had come to realize that Richard was constantly stuck in the past, present, *and* future. Richard had grown into adulthood around the fact that his father had disappeared and was never coming back, but Richard could talk about his father like they had just seen each other the day before.

The sad feeling when Mark remembered the nearly empty church just before his Gran was put in the ground was similar to what was completely worn into Richard's psyche. For a twenty-four-year-old, Richard was one of the hardest people he had ever met. Like Mark, Richard had very little fat on him. There was a key difference–Richard's body was filled out by wiry muscle.

One time when they were in the Rud (the bar that he, Richard, and Old Dirge usually drank at) Richard had got in a fight with a guy who had been loudly saying dirty things about the women in the bar. Richard had a habit of going off on massive diatribes, which Mark didn't mind for the most part. Even though it could be tiring at times, one of Richard's favorite subjects was (as best that Mark could sum it up): "How awful and pathetic most dragoons are when they are trying to, as Old Dirge puts it, 'get their dick wet.'"

Mark wasn't much for getting angry, but the guy Richard ended up fighting was taking it to a whole new level. It was enough that even Mark became angry. The guy was loudly comparing the boobs and butts of every girl in the room to how they compared to the size of fruits or different cuts of meat. When the guy finally got to 'grapefruits and top sirloin', the man grabbed at one of the women. Richard was on him in a second.

It scared Mark because he was not one for confrontation,

but Richard's familiar belligerent frustration dissipated and was replaced by blind fury and accompanied by coursing muscles and popping veins:

Grabbing the guy by the collar, Richard screamed directly to his face; "Get the FUCK out of here before I splatter your god-damned shitbrain all over the fucking bar!" He shook the man for emphasis. The man went to push Richard away and it was the excuse Richard needed to smash his fist into the guy's jawbone. Mark would not have guessed Richard could hit somebody that hard, but it had done the trick. The guy let out a painful yell, Richard had almost certainly broken his jaw.

The guy should have probably quit there, but decided to try to throw a punch into Richard's rib. Richard didn't even flinch and grabbed the guy by the wrist. Richard hit him straight in the chest with his free hand, which caused the guy to double over. As the guy was gasping for breath, Richard grabbed him by the collar, dragged him to the door, and threw him on the ground.

Richard had turned his back and started walking back to the bar. The guy got off the ground and turned to fight back in earnest. He ran at Richard and punched Richard in the back of the head. Rather than stopping Richard, it seemed to pull Richard's eyes into even more focus. Before the guy knew what was happening; Richard turned around, grabbed the top of the guy's head, and brought it down to meet his knee. The man slumped into a pile on the floor.

There was dead silence and for a second, Mark believed that Richard had killed him. The look on Richard's face said that he also thought he had killed the man.

The man let out a dull moan and the entire bar, who had watched most of the altercation intently, breathed a sigh of relief. Old Dirge brought the scene back to reality, "Help me throw him to the curb boys, this whistle dick doesn't deserve to wake up in here."

Richard and Old Dirge were good friends, friends that Mark knew would stand up for him no matter what.

Mark had finally made it into the building. He was glad to be out of the dark rain. It had begun to make the only coat he had, a present from his Gran for his sixteenth birthday, smell like a combination of farts and cleaning supplies.

He was also excited for class. Mark was actually a really good student. He was smart enough and got really good grades, but, as Richard had a habit of pointing out, mainly because it was easy. After trying to listen to Richard for a few hours, learning proper ways to talk to underlings was quite the mental vacation. He, unlike Richard, needed that. Well, he thought, Richard needed that too even if Richard didn't know it.

However, Mark was extra fearful whenever walking to this class. There was always this sports kid who would harass him whenever he walked by. Sometimes he pretended like he was about to chase Mark.

Mark hoped he would round the corner and the sports kid would be preoccupied trying to talk the short skirts off of girls. To his horror, there wasn't just the mean kid, there were a half dozen sports players and none of them were distracted by girls. The kid had spotted him walking towards them and got the attention of his teammates.

The sports kid played to his teammates, "Look at this little fag coming. Did you guys know he wears that same shitty jacket every single day? He looks like a fucking lazy bum." The laughter of the other sports kids encouraged him to walk all the way up to Mark.

Mark was filled with terror, a terror that could make one piss their pants. He looked around desperately. He was hoping that somebody would come to his rescue, but he didn't see any white night and prepared for a beating. There was no Richard, no Old Dirge, nor anybody else who would think of standing up to these hulks.

The kid shoved him into the wall. Mark had been shoved around plenty in his younger years, but the strength of the athlete (which was probably the result of carrying around too many extra pounds) made his shoulder blades sear with pain. Mark was on the verge of crying, but he didn't want to give the bullies the satisfaction. The other athletes circled around him with jeering stupid faces and began to harass him loudly all at once. He lost his nerve and began to whimper, begging them to let him go. His begging just caused them to laugh and get more sinister looks on their faces. Internally, Mark resigned himself to what he was about to have to endure. He looked around in desperation one more time and saw Richard step out of a nearby door.

Chapter 15

Richard's mind went into a blur. His friend was trapped by more dragoons than he would ever have the hope of fighting off and here, unlike the Rud, he would get in mountains of trouble. It didn't matter. Mark needed him and he was willing to get his lights punched out if it meant trying. He strode towards them ready to run headfirst into whoever turned around to see him first. A figure came running from the other direction. It was mean-ass Gregory.

Half a head taller and much more muscular, Gregory lifted one of the fatass sacks of shit off the ground and smashed his face into the wall. The kid crumpled and his nose began to pour blood. Gregory turned to the first kid who had accosted Mark, used his massive hand to grab the kid's head like a basketball, and (with precision) smashed his huge fist directly into the kid's temple. The kid fell straight to the ground unconscious.

Two of the semi-stunned players made an attempt to grab Gregory, neither had seen Richard coming. Richard came up behind them and tripped one of them backwards, shoulders over ankles, onto the ground. Gregory, in a flash of speed that would seem uncharacteristic to a giant, connected his picture perfect (nearly basketball) sized fist into the other one's sternum. The two others bolted in opposite directions. Looking down at the curled up 'athletes,' Richard couldn't help but feel a little pride-even though Gregory had done most of the work.

Richard's head eventually cleared from the fervor and a type of shock set in. He had always judged Gregory to be a mean bastard who would not be the kind of person to rush into a situation to defend someone like Mark. Richard had generally thought of Gregory as a bully, but it would seem like he was actually more a bully of bullies. It seemed absurd that the brooding giant would do such an altruistic thing. The memory of Gregory putting somebody through a door flashed through Richard's head. At the time, he assumed that Gregory was just being a bully. Now, he was pretty sure the person had deserved it. The whole notion that Richard had of Gregory prior to this was in stark contrast from the now smiling Giant.

Mark had not moved. Richard saw the terrified look on his friend's face and, in light of their victory, laughed.

The kid with the broken bleeding nose let out a low moan and began to crawl down the hallway. It elicited a feeling of pity from Richard, which was strange considering his hostile regard for his fucking joke of "*peers*". The player on the ground making a vacuum sound as he was slowly catching his breath was funny, but the bloody broken nose looked fairly serious. Still, picking on Mark was shitty enough that his pity stopped short of sympathy.

Mark and Richard both focused their attention on Gregory and his smiling relaxed demeanor. Both of them felt apprehension on top of a level of aftershock and terror, both were puzzled by Gregory's calm and relaxed demeanor.

Mark knew that he could get in trouble for just being here, even if he had been the one picked on. Richard knew that Mark shuffling from foot to foot meant he was obsessing over his fear of getting in trouble. The naive fear of reprimands was part of what gave Mark his enduring innocence, it was one of the things Richard really liked about Mark. Richard knew that Mark's innocence and fearful nature completely ruined his potential to lie and manipulate and that was one of the reasons Richard cared so deeply for his friend.

Richard also felt bad for Mark. He knew that Mark tried to be a model student and from what he understood–Mark certainly was. Richard had full confidence that Mark was absolutely smart enough to succeed in upper middle management, but Richard knew that no matter how hard Mark worked–he would never get there. The small frame, naive round face, and markedly poor clothing guaranteed that he would be in lower middle management forever.

As the last of the players (the one who had harassed Mark to the tune of a Gregory sized wrecking ball to the temple) got to his knees and began to crawl forward from the three standing victors, Gregory was the first to break the silence.

"What a bunch of losers." Gregory spit on the floor for dramatic effect, which further deviated from Richard's previous notion of him. Not only was he more calculated, he also seemed to have something of a sense of humor.

Gregory seemed to sense Mark's fear and Richard's confusion. Seemingly to keep the silence broken he cleared his throat in an obviously exaggerated way.

"Putting people like them in their place never ceases to give one a warm feeling. It is about the only thing that has kept me sane since I was a teenager. I love it, but this little stunt basically guarantees my one-way ticket out of this hellhole. Silver linings, right?"

Richard picked up on the pleasantry and loved the nonchalance.

In Richard's newfound admiration he had to chime in, "I

must say that I envy you. There are days I would love to have broken someone's nose just to be done with this goddamned cesspit. Shit man, that was quite the handiwork. How did you get that fast?"

"There are more people in this world that need a good pop to somewhere on their flab than you would believe, and I have always been one to oblige." Gregory replied, casually.

Richard was stunned. Just minutes ago he was being taught about how to smile at his underlings with the goal of making them more productive. Now here he was, having just come out on top of a scuffle, and talking to an obviously intelligent and compassionate Gregory. Richard's face broke into a genuine smile.

Richard turned to Mark, "You should probably head out of here, it is only a matter of time before someone or other shows up to tally up some unproductivity and I imagine that wouldn't bode well for you."

It broke Mark's shock and he quickly mumbled "thank you," before turning around and bolting towards the class he was now five minutes late for. It would seem strange to his classmates because Mark was always five minutes early. Mark wondered what his Gran would say, before blanking his mind because he was getting ready to learn to read the pie charts used in productivity and efficiency monitoring.

After Mark had disappeared around a corner, Gregory turned to Richard, "You probably want to follow your own advice."

Gregory sighed and looked directly at Richard in a level and clear way, "I really do want to be done with this place. It isn't exactly like I will ever be middle management material and I don't have a good track record of tolerating ignorance from *future leaders*." Richard loved that he had said *future leaders* in such an exaggerated and sarcastic tone.

Trying to play along Richard replied, "I know all too well. Most of these folks couldn't think themselves out of a cardboard box. I am not too partial to staying here either, except I suppose finding a place to live would be difficult. The power outages in the dorms are shitty and they are run down, but I can't even imagine what living in half of the crumbling buildings in the city would be like."

"There is no reason for you to get in trouble," Gregory said convincingly. "I'll take credit for the whole incident and deny that you were ever here."

Richard's mind suddenly flashed with the idea of sitting next to Mark and Gregory at the Rud, watching Old Dirge explore his kingdom. It was an image that made Richard smile harder.

"How do you feel about drinking a beer?" asked Richard.

"Very pro. One has to stay sane somehow, right?" Gregory said with an elegance and lightness that Richard would never have guessed out of, who he used to think of as, mean-ass Gregory.

Richard held onto his smile for a few moments before replying, "My sentiments exactly. Well, I do my drinking at The Rud most nights. Do you know it?"

"The Ruddy Irishman," Gregory laughed, "It had definitely been a while, it would be nostalgic to say the least."

Gregory reached his massive hand out for Richard to shake. Richard remembered what his father had taught him about shaking hands. He made a steady reach and firmly, but not tightly, grabbed Gregory's hand.

"It is a pleasure to finally meet you Richard," Gregory said with absolute sincerity.

"The pleasure is all mine Gregory," a phrase Richard had picked up from his father.

"I look forward to that drink, but you really should get out of here before I come to my senses about taking all the responsibility." Gregory laughed in a surprisingly light and charismatic way before bidding Richard to, "Take care of yourself until we meet again." There was something strangely calming about how Gregory was posturing himself.

Richard muttered, "See you soon," before turning and walking quickly towards his dorm. The daunting rain awaited him, but he didn't care at this point. For the second time in a long time, he might have made a friend.

Chapter 16

For the fourth night in a row, Mark found himself sitting at a table at The Rud with Richard and Gregory. He had never seen Richard in high spirits for so long. Since Gregory had started to come out to the Rud with them regularly, Richard became less prone to bouts of his brooding. If Mark had to guess, it was that having drunken conversations with somebody else who thought the world was run by shit brains relieved some of Richard's angst.

Richard knew quite a bit about quite a bit, but Gregory knew even more about what was going on in the city and why. Mark sometimes had a hard time following their conversations, but it wasn't just him. Whenever they got to talking, Old Dirge would almost always say "too rich for my old bones" and amble off to rule his kingdom from a different spot of the bar.

Mark sat through a lot of it to be a good friend, but he also did learn quite a bit, as both Richard and Gregory had a way of explaining things that was much better than his lower-middle management teachers. It was fun for him to see his friend light up and talk without swearing belligerently for long periods of time. Mark had already liked Richard before, but he really liked the new Richard that seemed to have some type of newfound energy. He was also very much starting to like Gregory too.

Gregory had a laugh-in-the-face-of-danger-attitude that he wore on his sleeves. On top of that, Gregory did it in a way that would loosen up a room. Mark noticed that people smiled more openly when Gregory would speak to them. Mark could never believe it when Gregory would just plop down at random tables and have hour-long conversations. What baffled Mark even more was that Richard had started to join Gregory.

Not that long ago Richard would snap at just about anybody who came near him, except Mark and Old Dirge. The few conversations he did get into would almost always end in a heated argument. Mark always had wanted to get along with people and to avoid confrontation at all costs. It had struck him a few nights back that Richard was every bit as reckless in conversations as Gregory claimed to be in life.

Mark believed Gregory whenever he spoke. His voice always came out with a tone of genuine sincerity and everything he said was believable. Mark suspected that Gregory had an underlying calculated reason for talking to people like he did.

Everything Mark had heard Gregory say had the same underlying 'cynicism towards the world' message that Richard always got stuck in. The difference was that Gregory could pull groups of people into caring, whereas Richard only seemed to succeed in getting into heated arguments with strangers. There were times, like the night Richard had marched Mark through the slums to go to the bar Richard's father had spoken at, that Richard could draw people in with his stories–but that was more of an exception than the rule.

Richard and Gregory hadn't been talking about politics all night long and Old Dirge had spent most of the night sitting at their table. Periodically he would get up and wander over to other patrons to trade a story for his next round. That was pretty much what Old Dirge did for a living, because drinking was his living. That and wander out a few hours each morning to pull old copper out of the walls of abandoned buildings. He only pulled as much as he needed in order to buy a questionably sanitary meal at the Rud before settling into a night of drinking. Old Dirge was funny like that.

The bar went silent, seemingly all at once. Mark looked over and saw five Citizen Watchers standing inside the doorway of the room.

Chapter 17

Halfway through his sentence, the entire room went quiet. Richard had his back facing the door so he couldn't see at first, but the look on Gregory's face went from jovial to extremely serious. He turned in his chair and immediately recognized the man who Old Dirge had so wonderfully smashed a mug on for picking on the 'outsiders'. This time the man wasn't wearing a flannel shirt, he was wearing a Citizen Watch uniform and was standing in front of four other Citizen Watchers. Richard didn't think many other people would make the connection, but he knew for damned sure that Old Dirge did. Just looking at Old Dirge, you could see the terror in him rising. Old Dirge was a tough old bastard, but five citizen watchers were there for him and that was more than Old Dirge could do anything about.

For some reason, Richard immediately thought of the girl with his mother's stars in her eyes who he had seen put down two of the brutes all by herself. If she would take a stand against these violent pseudo cops, then he certainly would do it for Old Dirge. Richard was afraid. He figured he would have no chance in the world of stopping five Watchers and would most likely end up with broken bones as well as in jail. His last physical encounter with Watchers didn't exactly leave him the better for it. Still, what the man in his Citizen Watcher uniform had done in the first place had been vile and what he was about to do to an old man was worse.

Before Richard could stir up the courage to get between the Watchers and Old Dirge, Gregory had gotten up from the table. Gregory had a burning look of anger on his face. All of the charm, calm, and allure he embodied when he was out drinking with Richard and Mark was replaced by concentration.

Richard was taken aback. Gregory didn't even know what they had come for and he was ready to stand down five Watchers, one clearly holding a baseball bat. Inspired by Gregory's courage, Richard rose to stand next to his new friend.

Richard watched the man Old Dirge had smashed with a mug look about the room. The bartender, a man who went by Lundy, shuffled over and tentatively asked them what they wanted. Most of what the man said was too far away for Richard to hear, but he clearly heard "old man." He looked over and saw Old Dirge seized up in a panic. Gregory must have heard it too, because he turned to Old Dirge. Richard could see in Gregory's eyes that he had pieced together the situation entirely, even though he had not been there for the initial altercation.

He turned to Richard and said, "I don't care what the old fuck did, I am not letting these assholes have their fun." Gregory quickly scoped the room and, to Richard's confusion, made a hand gesture before striding over to all five of them to laugh in the face of danger. Richard was so impressed with Gregory's bravery that he followed one step behind; the level of inspiration was so great that he had lost all fear. He didn't exactly know why, but he knew that Gregory could handle things.

When he and Gregory had come face to face with the five Watchers, they began to laugh. Richard's confidence ebbed, but he had already committed and he wasn't going back on it. Gregory was completely undaunted.

The Watcher there for old dirge spoke up, "What do you think you're doing boys? We got business here and we don't mind doing it over your bloody corpse."

The bar was in total silence waiting for him or Gregory to speak. Richard turned to his friend and saw confidence radiating from him. His admiration for his friend flared and he decided to stand proud and look at the Watchers face to face.

Gregory looked the man right in the eyes and said audibly, "Why don't you piss off, before you piss me off."

The silence in the room focused on the two young men standing down grown Watchers. Every ear that had been listening listened closer, the entire room was overcome with fear. Richard thought he heard the shuffling of footsteps behind him. He couldn't be sure because of how focused he was on how much pain he was about to be in. 'If they kill me, at least I won't have to deal with Janis anymore,' he thought sarcastically.

The look of smug authority on the Watcher's face had been replaced by flushed red cheeks and wore the disdain of insulted pride.

"What did you say to me Boy? Make sure you speak up, these words might well be your last," he had tried to say *last* with an ominous snarling sound, but his voice had faltered.

Gregory, who hadn't taken his eyes off the man's face, repeated in a patronizing manner, slowly and word by word; "Piss. Off. Before. You. Piss. *Me*. Off. Are we clear?"

The man started towards Gregory. Richard saw Gregory's hand twitch and the man's head snap backwards as he free-fell to the floor. If the man wasn't dead, it was a miracle. The silence in the room was a vacuum for a second before being broken by footsteps behind them. Four young men brushed past Richard to stand at their side. It didn't seem like random acts of bravery. The Watcher with the bat stepped forward as his friends tended to their probably dead friend.

Two of Gregory's friends stepped forward, which was the excuse the man had been waiting for to use his bat. He hadn't gotten halfway through the swing before one of them grabbed onto his arm and the other kneed him in the stomach.

One of the Watchers stood up and in a scared imitation of an authoritative voice tried to command, "We are Watchers! You can't do this." He turned to one of the other Watchers and told him to send for the police.

Gregory stepped towards them and stated with a perfect air of authority, "Your man unknowingly assaulted the son of a general in the army you little shits got kicked out of. For that, I will let the rest of you leave with your bones intact. If you make any mention of this to your handlers, you will have shit piled onto your head until you drown in it. Are we clear? Because your friend wasn't and I would hate for you to have to join him." The Watchers all had extreme looks of horror on their faces and, after exchanging rapid glances, they raced out the door leaving their probably dead comrade lying on the floor. Old Dirge was on Gregory in a second begging him gratitude.

Gregory turned to his comrades who had appeared out of

nowhere and said in a half-whisper to them; "Drag him a few blocks away, strip off his uniform, and toss him into a dumpster." One grabbed the man's legs, the other grabbed his arms, and they shuffled out the door. Every person in the bar was in complete disbelief.

Chapter 18

Richard was just short of being close-one-eye-to-see-straight-drunk. Everyone in the bar, who hours before had sat in silent horror, had warmed up considerably. If Old Dirge was a hero, then Gregory was a legend and nobody at the table paid for a drink all night

Old Dirge was in the highest spirits Richard had ever seen. It seemed as if there was a genuine spark in him. 'It's easy when you narrowly escape death,' Richard thought to himself. Old Dirge was usually flamboyantly happy, but Richard could tell it was an act most of the time. An act in order to get people to pay for the drinks he couldn't afford on his copper salvaging money.

It was almost like Old Dirge's eyes had lit up and he had

suddenly become alive. Over the course of the night, he had drunkenly swore to both Richard and Gregory that he would never walk away from one of their conversations again. It was strange, but Richard actually believed him. Gregory had a strange way of affecting people and he had certainly won over The King of the Rud.

Gregory was without a doubt the strangest person Richard had ever met. After the quick words whispered to his friends, neither of whom had returned, Gregory hadn't said a word about it. Periodically, young men in varying states of drunk, had wandered over to shake Gregory's hand and to tell him how much they supported what he did.

What they said didn't sit well with Richard. Unlike Old Dirge, who now seemed to have a genuine interest in wanting to know more about the young man who (more or less) saved his life, these people seemed to come over to be seen coming over. After talking to Gregory, they would return to their corner of the bar so that girls could huddle excitedly and ask their now brave suitor just how brave Gregory was. 'Taking credit through professed solidarity in order to get your dick wet, how much more shitbrained can you get?' Richard thought.

Oddly enough, Gregory had even calmed a fair amount of Mark's skittishness. After Richard had gotten in the fight with the drunken ass grabber, Mark had teetered on whimpering for the rest of the night. The same sincere admiration that came from Old Dirge was visible in Mark as well. Richard imagined that Mark too was probably radiating from Gregory's presence. His drunken endearment for his mousy friend rose in him.

Richard knew that he could be a hard person to be around most of the time. Even Janis barely tolerated him long enough for what, he had to imagine, was the most unsatisfying orgasm in the world. She always tried to hide it. Sometimes she would just repeat *yes* over and over until his dick went limp. It was unfathomable to him how somebody who hated him as much as she did could go so rabid for him the instant she snaked her hand down into his pants. For Richard to actually get off, he had to think about literally anything else.

As far as Richard could see, Mark had no reason to be around him. Other than drinks here and there, it wasn't like Mark got anything out of their friendship–drinks that usually came with a hangover for Mark. He supposed that it might be that they were just two loners together.

Whatever it was or wasn't, they had a great friendship. Before Mark came along, he had actually given up and resigned himself to loneliness. Alone in the world, but with Janis. Richard looked back and forth between Mark and Gregory, he was certainly not alone in the world anymore and things were looking up.

The remaining two friends of Gregory (who had seemingly appeared out of nowhere) had kept to themselves for the most part, even though they had joined the table. They talked in quiet voices. At one point Richard had tried to listen in to what they were saying, but he was drunk and they didn't seem overly eager to have him participate. In all the revelry, the question of who the four young men were or where they came from (obviously they had just been sitting at a different table) kept burning in his head. With the way that Gregory had moved on in complete nonchalance, it hadn't left time for Richard to ask him.

Richard sometimes read the newspaper and a story he had recently read continued to cross his mind. It hadn't been from the Liberty Standard, the main newspaper distributed by the government, but from a local paper he found at a coffee shop in easy walking distance from his dorm. The story hadn't been the headline and he only found it by combing through the entire paper, but it claimed that young former military personnel who were unaffiliated with the Citizen Watchers or Police had begun to be seen in numbers throughout town. As Richard looked at the two of Gregory's friends sitting in relative silence, he did notice a uniformity in hair length and movement. He was skeptical to draw conclusions but, in light of the evening's earlier events–anything seemed plausible.

Gregory walked over to Richard, sat down next to him, and

asked, "You mind if I bum a smoke?"

It took Richard aback for a moment, "I didn't know you smoked."

Gregory flashed a knowing smile, "Sometimes when I drink. Want to step out?" Then he got up and stepped towards the door.

Richard was more than happy to oblige. Neither Mark nor Old Dirge ever smoked, so he always felt like the odd man out every time he would relieve the itch of the raspy cough by going outside and lighting up a cigarette.

There was apprehension in Richard about stepping outside. A fear overtook him that there would be a mob of Watchers waiting for them outside the door, but it quickly went away because he realized that Gregory had probably already thought about that and it seemed to him like Gregory could handle nearly any situation.

When he got outside, he felt hot dry night air. The kind that came with a heat wave. Gregory felt it too. He turned and joked, "I'm going to have to start sleeping in the nude again, so I'll get to thank the heat for that." Then added for Richard's benefit, "If those shitbrains had just done something when they started talking about this almost a century ago, eh?" He motioned for a cigarette.

Richard handed him one and dug for matches in his pocket, but before he found them, Gregory flipped out a lighter in a metal case and lit it with zeal in the way Richard had seen movie stars do when he was little. Gregory never ceased to impress.

As Richard lit his own, Gregory began, "I suppose I am not entirely the person you thought I was. Before you found me in that hellhole you unfortunately still live in, I had an interesting life. At eighteen I told my father to shove it, but the military was in my blood. I joined the most dangerous corps they would let me into just to disappoint my father for not aiming for something that would lead me down his path someday.

It was all fine and dandy in training, but when I saw what was really happening out in the world, I couldn't do it. Rather than just quit, I requested a break from my contract to go learn to be a more effective officer candidate and naturally with my father being a General, I got it. When I finally got into the Management Academy, nothing I saw there was any better. Middle Managers are every bit as responsible for the horrors going on around every day as the people who commit them. Obviously, you were there to see how my venture in middle management ended."

He paused to look Richard up and down before leaning in to say, "I have some friends who want to make a difference in the world that might interest you and I'm wondering if you would maybe like to meet them?"

Richard was totally taken aback and not knowing what to do

or considering what he might be in for, he immediately agreed to it. Gregory unceremoniously handed him a slip of paper with a handwritten address, date, and time, before flicking his half-finished cigarette into the street and walking back into the bar. Richard was in awe and reverence. Maybe for the first time in his life, somebody might help him make a difference.

Chapter 19

It was a miracle; Richard had already begun to sober up before the night was over. He was so swept up thinking about what Gregory might have just asked him to do that he had forgotten to keep slamming drinks. At one point he had even tried to strike up an awkward conversation with the two newly met strangers who had rushed past him to defend Old Dirge, in the hopes that something they might say would give him an idea about what the piece of paper he had just gotten meant.

Richard wasn't very good at conversations and even worse at friendly ones; his pleasantries were noticeably forced and after a minute or two of generic questions about their life and background, followed by short answers, then awkward silences, he gave up and decided just to take in the electric atmosphere.

There was an air of *justice-served* all about the room, because the Citizen Watchers were not popular amongst the majority of people. It seemed like the onlookers in the bar, all who in some way realized that the world was a messed-up place, were brought joy to see somebody suffer who *actually* deserved it.

Throughout the evening, he had heard an abnormal amount of glasses being clinked together as people proclaimed solidarity and imitated the revelry they imagined was felt by Gregory and his comrades.

Every time Richard heard the clinking of glasses, muscles all over his body tensed up in anticipation that he might learn the truth of the revelry they actually shared. The anticipation was only heightened by the fact that Gregory hadn't made any type of acknowledgment that their conversation outside had even occurred. Every so often, Richard had found himself reaching down into his pocket to make sure the piece of paper Gregory handed him was still there.

He had tried to tell Mark, but Mark was nearly at close-one-eye-just-to-see-straight-drunk and had been caught up with all the people coming over to talk to them and Gregory. Mark was giddy and excitable, something Richard had rarely seen. The usually timid mousiness was replaced by an upbeat sense of security.

It wasn't as though Mark was sticking out his chest or pretending to have rushed to Gregory's side, but that he felt safe around his new friend. The same reassuring feeling that Gregory gave off which caused Richard to follow right behind him to face the Watchers had also temporarily calmed Mark's fears of the world.

The only times Richard had seen this many people in a room act this carefree and animated had been the times when his parents' friends had come to his parents' house for dinner. His father would radiate the same confidence that wore so thick on Gregory. They were entirely different people, but people's reactions to them were strikingly similar.

Richard's father had been an amazing man. He could captivate anybody in a room, but nobody more so than his mother. The starry eyes of the, what he could remember, fairly beautiful girl he had met facedown in an alley flashed through his mind. When he was very little, his mother had them all the time. Sometimes his father had been gone for weeks at a time and yet Richard's mother would still have them, which stood in stark contrast to most of his teenage years where the stars had faded.

After his father had been taken away, he could only remember one time where her eyes had lit up like they did when he was younger. Even with the revelry going on around him, he stared off into space and allowed his mind to wander back to the last time that he had seen his mother happy:

He was sixteen and had tested highly for college potential. It was a few clicks away from being perfect, but still one of the best that his school counselor had seen. After the scores came back, he sat in Mr. Allison's office while a number of future plans were laid in front of him. From the onset–Mr. Allison had made it clear that while it was quite the accomplishment to score a high score, Richard had fallen short of the perfect record he would have needed at their school to get into some of the more prestigious schools. Richard hadn't taken any offense; prior to sitting there, he hadn't given much serious thought to what he would do with his life.

The problem that kept popping up whenever Richard would think about the future was the finite sense of purpose that he imagined followed making a life decision. This was further compounded by the fact that he had scored well across the board, nothing stood out more than any other. Management, infrastructure, clerical, and skilled labor scores not differentiating by much, but all markedly above average.

He was sold on the dutiful responsibility of management, the brilliant calculations involved in engineering and maintaining infrastructure, the satisfaction of a task done right when combing over anything that required clerical insight, or the sense of fulfillment after a hard day of skilled labor. At the moment, they all seemed equally appealing.

His mother sat beside him. In an attempt to inspire family zeal towards a finite goal, parents had been invited to come in and hear the possible future of their children. It was like a tarot reading, but from standard test scores. His mother had come painstakingly. It wasn't as though she didn't want to be there, she had just been sick for quite a while at that point.

His mother had been skinny for a while, but it had gotten to a point that had made her movements laborious. This time she had come down from a mild case of pneumonia and had a raspy cough that took him several years to match. She had resisted any effort to get help beyond going to see her personal doctor. Shortly before, he had sat in a room at his mother's doctor's office while his mother's doctor told his mother that moving around too much could cause exhaustion. She hadn't seemed to care, she was more excited than he was to hear the news about his future. The exhaustion, amongst a few other things, would eventually kill her– but he would never forget seeing the last spark that he ever saw in her.

Richard was sold time and time again, but before too long his mother had interceded; "If he is well above average," she paused, "then wouldn't he get the most out of the Management or Infrastructure programs?"

The counselor smiled and nodded in agreement. He plucked away at a worn-out keyboard on the internet that would soon become unreliable to all but a few, "There are quite a few programs that might fit that. So, Richard, do you want to hear about management or infrastructure or both?"

"I suppose I don't know," was all Richard replied.

Mr. Allison looked at his mother, probingly, for a more suitable answer. She looked at him before turning to Mr. Allison and answering rhetorically, "Why not hear about both?"

Mr. Allison donned a look of fraternal patience, the kind of patience given to those with an appointment; "We can certainly do both. Let me take a look." He paused momentarily, "I suppose I will start with industry." He paused again, as if for dramatic effect. '*Most people must love this*,' Richard thought. Still, he would make good of it because his mother looked happier than he had seen her in years.

"There are quite a few options to consider. Your scores are short of some of the better engineering tracks, but there is a wonderful career to be had in mid-level engineering." Richard bristled at the word *career*. "The calculations they do, as best as I understand them, are pretty routine. Having said that, you do get the chance to work on different projects all the time. The salary is pretty comfortable too. With your scores you would probably be bumped into the upper middle engineering category, which just makes the job a little more interesting and pays slightly better."

It hadn't sounded any worse than other things he had thought of possibly doing. He faked interest and asked, "So where would I go to do that?"

"There are quite a few options in the city. A few outside as well, but it gets expensive and you don't get anything more for it. It's an option, but I tend to encourage students to make smarter choices about where they spend their money on school."

"Are any of them better than the others?" Richard shot back, not considering his tone.

Mr. Allison looked at him and then his mother before lowering his voice to an almost whisper as if he was about to tell some type of guarded secret; "They are all exactly the same. Down to each individual assignment, they are exactly the same. I suppose some teachers are better than others, but it's really just one of things you have to just get through. It hardly matters later what you were taught or who taught it. The cheaper the better, right?"

The sentiment was all too familiar. His whole life people like Mr. Allison had reasoned with him, always in the same 'listen to my wisdom' tone, that everything he had to do in life was in fact bullshit. The strangest thing was how it then turned into a selling point. The selling point had become more and more hollow every time Richard got to what was supposed to be the reprieve on the other side. It seemed as if the further he got in the system, the more

145

bullshit there was.

"Money isn't really the issue, but if they are all the same you have a point," his mother responded when he didn't. Richard was bothered a bit that the idea of a completely uniform education didn't even make her slightly twinge. The idea of an education void of individuality or exploration of thought *certainly* bothered him.

"I think I would probably be more interested in management." Richard said frankly.

Mr. Allison gave an elongated "Ahhhhhh" and then an "O-K", with each letter pronounced separately, he was looking pronounced. 'People must *really* love this,' Richard thought.

"There is a perfect upper-middle management school only a few districts over. They teach out of their district mostly, but they are always looking for promising upper-middle management students. You are even a few points higher than their requirement. You would get into the program no problem." It was a sales pitch that almost sounded like Mr. Allison had an incentive to enroll him in the program. Richard stopped being cynical for a moment, figuring that Mr. Allison didn't see students like him every day.

"It is run by the Academy of Middle Management Company. Their upper middle managers are known for their ability to climb the ladder; a full 15% average increase in pay, they say. Everybody has to climb ladders, might as well do it in management, right?" Richard was as sold as he had ever been.

"The Academy of Middle Management," his mother said knowingly, "is a fairly good school from what I've heard."

For a moment he had seen a spark in her. She looked over to him and for the first time wore a trace of the gaze she would give his father. He had felt truly proud of himself at that moment. Even though the test hadn't been that hard, he had apparently gotten a really good score. At least he wasn't entirely crazy when he felt that he was smarter than a lot of people.

Gregory and his friends were leaving. After Gregory made his rounds to shake hands with a half dozen people, he doubled back to say his goodbyes for the night to Richard, Mark, and Old Dirge. After Old Dirge's final display of gratitude (wringing Gregory's hand for what seemed like a whole minute), Gregory told Mark to 'keep his head up,' before turning to Richard and knowingly saying, "I imagine I will be seeing you soon." With near military cadence, Gregory and his two friends marched out the door.

Both Old Dirge and Mark looked at Richard quizzically. He debated telling them both about the earlier conversation outside on the spot, but Old Dirge was extremely drunk and would have to be told multiple times, which didn't even guarantee he would remember any of it in the morning. It was also late and Richard was tired.

"I will tell you later. I'm going to head back, I'm tired and it looks like the hangover might start early." Mark's face showed agreement. Mark was nowhere near as drunk as he had been a few hours before and looked tired in alcohol's wake.

Old Dirge bid adieu, "Have a good night boys. I'm going to stay here and make good on the evening. I can't pass up free drinks, no sir."

With none of the fanfare of Gregory's departure, Richard and Mark left the bar.

Chapter 20

Richard had followed Gregory's note to the place and location on it at the time it had specified; he had even convinced Mark to join him in the adventure. When they got there, there was an entire room full of young people. Many had the military look of the four friends of Gregory's who had rushed to defend Old Dirge from the Citizen Watchers, but there were plenty of normal-looking people as well. There were plenty of girls, some with the military look and some without.

Richard could see Gregory standing near a podium on a crudely constructed stage because this was clearly an abandoned building. The sound of the Generators that were being used to light the room and power the speakers could be heard in the background. Richard didn't want to push his way through the crowd to try to talk to his new friend because Gregory was obviously about to deliver something powerful and he knew he would only be a distraction.

Gregory looked down and then looked up at the large crowd gathered in front of him. He knew he had to be absolutely on point, but if he could do it—he knew his words would change at least a small corner of the world. He took solace in that. What he was feeling in his heart was true and the time was here to speak the truth about what he knew to anyone who would listen.

He walked up to the podium and cleared his throat, waiting for the crowd to silence. The crowd turned attentively and he started into his speech:

"A lot of you likely don't remember what things were like in the time before this decrepit world, before we got to this point of no return. That is exactly what this is. The time we're in is a point of no return. Believe it or not, the world hasn't always been this way. Things were better in previous times. Every period in human history has had their own type of suffering. Humanity has always suffered, but not like this. This suffering is completely avoidable.

What we are seeing is what happens when humanity believes that it is lost. We're living in a time when the path of a very select group of people is completely separate from what almost all of the others are walking. The world looks entirely different depending on your privilege. You are all here because you see the disparity in our situation.

It doesn't have to be like this. We have to do something. But, first, why *are* you here? What does being here mean to *you*?" Gregory paused for a moment, taking a sip of his drink and looking at the very back of the audience, noting just how many people were in the room. He began again:

"We live in a world with constant suffering. And not just some of us, but nearly everyone. This suffering, as dark as it might feel, can bring us together. Nearly every one of us has known someone who has died because of the ills of our time, but all of us are still here, and I think there's a reason for it. It's not just by chance, even if it feels like it at times.

Now, this may seem odd, but the truth often does. Not my truth, not your truth, but everyone's. You all are stronger than you even realize. You're not just strong because you have a curiosity, you are strong because you recognize the real dangers of our world for what they are. We didn't make up the dangers, we just know them. Many of us have studied them. We certainly have lived them. Something happened that has led to the decay of society. What happened, you may ask?

People got comfortable. The dangers of the world are

obvious to us and I can't promise you that they won't always be there. But, the immediacy the average person felt and the desire to act died years ago. Some got rich, very rich, while others got complacent and apathy corrupted their will to address the all too real problems that led us to where we are today.

Most people ignore some of our world's threats and believe they can listen to what our leaders want them to do, even as the same leaders rob everyone blind. Our leaders can only rob us blind because they feel safe. It's bullshit, but that's how they feel. Money, power, influence, political maneuvers all stem from a basic idea—make people too scared or too comfortable to challenge the system to make it better. They gave up on making people too comfortable a long time ago.

We don't all have to acknowledge the same basic dangers. Sometimes at first, it won't feel natural. We are accustomed to accepting reality in the same ways as our neighbors because that's what people do, why be different?

I will tell you this. We have to be different because if we don't, then nothing will ever change. The rich will keep getting richer and the poor will keep getting poorer. If you look out your windows at night you all know this is about as far into that pit of inequality that we could fall into. Reality, itself, has started losing relevance. More people than not who are suffering at this moment, deny their own reality.

This collapsed society came to be because people started becoming apathetic. They started accepting that instead of saying 'we need to work together, we need to live these truths that are self-evident, we need to help our fellow person'-they just said, 'I don't think we can, so we won't.' That very apathy, an apathy that started small, built up over time and then kept on building. When poverty came for people's neighbors, people just looked the other way.

Reality can be whatever you want if you have the money and the influence. You can perpetuate that reality for as long as you want, even as the world crumbles around you. Where does that leave the common person? We live in a world where it takes everything in their power just for a family to survive. My own father got swept up in it and he serves the system. But now I'm here, with you, speaking my truth that we're not going to let this take us down forever.

We can fight-and we will. We're going to be the ones to change the world. I know it and I hope you know it too. I've spent enough time around my father's powerful friends to know that they are scared shitless of what we're capable of doing if we come together. They created the Citizen Watchers to stop us from ever congregating in public. Let's show them that they are wrong.

I have a number of weapons and anyone who wants to wield one, can. However, this is not a call to open revolution. In just our lifetimes, the government has changed the rules of food distribution as a means of control. It is no accident nor oversight that the rations system was put in place and was directly tied to your job as well as your position within the ruling class. There is no true shortage of food, it is being used as a means of control.

We will strike out at this tool of the elite-like the Robin Hood of old, we will steal from the rich and give to the poor. We'll take the fight to them and we will rewrite the narrative by putting the poorest first in our sympathies. There's more of us than there are of them and if we are all on the same page together, they can not beat us. We must all be aware of the dangers, but we also have a moral imperative to accept that danger. If we do not do this, then who will? If we do not win now, will there ever be a time when those that come after us have a better hope? We are the last line of defense. So, what do you say? Will you fight with us? Let us unite! Let us make history!"

Gregory stepped away from the podium to a thundering applause. The speech clearly resonated with the crowd. Gregory had notes before the speech that he could look at if he got hung up, but he hadn't had to look at them a single time. He had spoken the truth and a fire had been lit. He was starting a movement and it was about to change everything.

Richard looked out and saw a girl approaching Gregory's side of the stage. The sight of her hit him like a freight train: it was the girl from the alleyways. 'Oh my god, that's her. That's the girl with the stars in her eyes,' he thought to himself.

Richard also approached the stage. Seeing Richard, Gregory made straight for him to shake his hand. Gregory turned and pointed at the girl from the alleyway, "Richard, my friend, have you met my sister Rhia? Rhia, this is Richard. We've become something of comrades as of late."

Gregory waved to someone else in the crowd and told the two that he has to go shake some hands but that he'll catch up with them at The Rud later on.

After a short and awkward silence Richard blurted out, "You're the woman from the alleyway, aren't you?"

She replied glibly, "Obviously you know that, because you're the guy from the alleyway."

Richard motioned to the door. "I'm not much for a crowded room of people who aren't just trying to get drunk and I don't know very many people here, would you want to join me at The Rud? Apparently, your brother will join us when he is done shaking all of these hands."

Richard and Rhia's eyes locked for a moment that seemed to last for hours, but in reality, was just a few seconds. Both of them could feel an extreme connection between each other, but neither knew why. Rhia was curious enough that she agreed.

The two walked to The Rud, chatting casually the whole way.

Once there, Richard gave Rhia a quick glance and felt something more intense than either times he had run into her in the alleyways. She was a very beautiful girl, but this wasn't mere physical attraction. He had a deep and sincere curiosity about her and her story.

She had the same kind of angst that he and Gregory shared radiating off of her, yet hers had the same type of inspirational pull as her brothers'. Much like her brother, she had a natural presence. She obviously had the same kind of ingrained bravery that Gregory did, considering she put herself in constant danger by taking on the violent Citizen Watchers. Richard was hooked.

Sensing an awkward pause coming he asked, "Rhia, that's a unique name, who were you named after?"

She smiled and replied, "Rhia is short for Rhiannon. It's an old song you have probably heard as well as a Celtic Goddess." Richard had a vague recollection of his parents playing it.

He smiled back, "I remember hearing it a long time ago, back when there were more radio stations and you didn't need batteries to power radios more than half the time. I'm not sure I could remember two lines of it now though, it was a while ago. The Celtic Goddess thing is very cool."

She winked at him, "Probably not in a crowded dive bar, but I could sing it for you sometime if you would like?"

Richard had just begun to think of some type of clever reply, but Gregory and a handful of other people from the rally burst noisily through the door. Mark was a few feet behind him. Richard felt a twinge of guilt at having left his friend behind, but the look on Mark's face clearly showed that he did not mind. Gregory spotted them at once and made straight for their table. Before Gregory sat down he looked at the two of them and laughed. He raised his eyebrows a few times in a knowing sort of way. Both Rhia and Richard immediately blushed.

Gregory, Mark, and the other people from the rally all sat down and started drinking the night away. It felt as if there was a jolt of power bouncing between the group. They started off talking about the details of what Gregory had proposed, but it eventually turned into half a dozen separate conversations where they were all just exchanging stories about their lives and experiences. It was a type of comradery that Richard had never felt before in his life. Best of all, he was sitting next to Rhia and even when they weren't directly talking to each other they were exchanging glances.

The darkness had eased, even for a day. Outside, the wind kicked up-change had arrived.

Chapter 21

She traveled alone through a run-down district, keeping her ears open for the first hint of an approaching group of Citizen Watchers. She understood the Citizen Watchers, they were a tool of the people that she had so often had to interact with. Her brother's assessment that they were just criminal rejects of the formal military and police systems held true through all of her encounters. He was also right that they were cowards and bullies who would run at the first sight of real danger. The thought of the hysterical way they reacted to being jumped by a girl never failed to get a smile out of her.

Unfortunately, in a district like this, she also knew that there could be gangs running around acting similar to Citizen Watchers. She also understood gangs; if a person can't make it in a world because it has shut you out, it is only logical that a person would resort to whatever means necessary to stay alive. Understanding their plight was one thing, dealing with them was (unfortunately) a completely different story. She was not prone to fear, but the address her brother had given her was in a district that she had rarely visited. She was plenty resourceful and fear would do her no good anyway, so she kept her ears sharp and let her mind wander.

It had been something of an answer to her prayers, because even her vigilantism had begun to excite her less and less. Her brother had one of his military friends, who was paraded in front of her like the rest of the boys courting the General's daughter, pass her a note from him. The note was short and simple.

"Rhia,

I am going to speak in front of a handpicked group of people about the change we talk about. I think you need to hear it.

Love,

Your only and favorite brother." The only other details were the time, date, and location.

She knew her brother well. He was hot-headed at times (especially in his earlier years), but his ability to be charismatic had grown considerably since then and was undeniable. Between his size and the intonations in his voice when he spoke passionately, he had, in earlier years, even caused some of the elites at her father's parties to question the nature of the system that they were so devoted to. If Gregory promised her a speech that could cause change, he likely had the ability to do it.

She snapped back to her current surroundings. Her success at terrorizing the Citizen Watchers was because she had learned the landscape of several districts and was excellent at ambushing them. The district she was in now did not give her that advantage. There was a fear of the unknown in every shadow. Still, she had her wits and was extremely interested in hearing her brother speak–so she suppressed her reservations and pressed on through the night.

When she finally arrived at the location from the note, she found an extremely crowded room. She arrived early, but apparently her brother had riled up quite a few people. She searched the crowd for familiar faces.

Her brother was already near the podium he was going to speak from. His military friends, a few of which had already been paraded in front of her, stood guard between him and the crowd. She could absolutely feel the energy and excitement going throughout the room. She knew this was the exact situation he thrived on.

Turning away from the somewhat familiar faces that lined

the stage, she caught a glimpse of the young man she had crashed into in the alleyway. The hair on the back of her neck stood straight up. This was the third time she had seen him, all in completely different districts (the fourth if the shadow in the alleyway the night she had fought the citizen watchers to save the homeless woman wasn't a figment of her imagination or a trick of the light). There was a crowd of people between them and she figured that she would not have time to talk to him before her brother's speech, so she turned and waited for her brother to begin.

She could tell her brother was especially confident, but when he finally spoke–she was not expecting how much it would resonate. She, an intellectual sparring partner of his, had heard his ideas in rough forms over the years–but he had definitely put them together in a way that was clearly stirring something in the people around her. Her brother had clearly found his voice; she even found herself caught up by words that she had heard before.

Immediately after the speech, she rushed through the crowd to congratulate her brother. Strange became stranger though, because out of the corner of her eye she saw the stranger from the alleyway doing the same. Gregory saw them both before either made it up to where he was standing and, to her surprise, greeted his friend before her.

Turning to Rhia, Gregory asked his friend, "Richard, my friend, have you met my sister Rhia? Rhia, this is Richard. He and

I have become something of comrades as of late."

She was shocked for several reasons. First off, for most of her life Gregory had fully committed to the protective brother role and had run off several suitors that she actually liked. Second is that he never spoke highly of nearly anyone, not even most of his friends. Lastly, because she knew him well, she could tell he was subtly signaling to her that Richard was a person she might actually be interested in. It all seemed to be too much of a coincidence. Then Gregory just walked off to let them talk, something she had never in a million years expected to see her brother to do.

There was an awkward silence at first, she could see in Richard's face that he was just as blown away by the turn of events as she was. After a short amount of small talk, he asked her if she wanted to get out of the crowded room (something she had come to detest as of late) and, out of curiosity as much as anything, she obliged. She typically wouldn't go on a walk with a random person, but she sensed no ulterior motive from him. Plus, the way her brother had spoken about him meant he was interesting and that intrigued her.

The district between the meeting place and the bar they were going to was not overly run down, so the likelihood of running into trouble wasn't nearly as high as her trip to the meeting place. She liked that he had a dark sense of humor. He had a genuine way of making her laugh. At times, she sensed that he was a little nervous and was using humor to mask it. It didn't exactly bother her because she was actually a little nervous as well. The whole situation felt surreal and almost too coincidental to be real.

Once they got to The Rud, Richard pointed at a fairly large open table and said, "I have a feeling that we will have more joining us than just Gregory and Mark. Shit, I forgot about Mark." Richard's cheeks flushed a little bit.

Rhia laughed and put her hand on his shoulder, "I wouldn't worry too much, my brother won't leave him behind." Richard laughed too, realizing that Gregory would obviously take care of Mark.

They ordered drinks which, despite her protests, Richard insisted on buying and went over to sit at the large table. There was a pause once they sat down. Both were exchanging glances not knowing exactly where to start the conversation back up. Richard asked her a bit about herself, but the conversation was cut short by the arrival of her brother and a mob of his followers, including Mark. She looked over at Richard and could see the relief on his face that his friend was amongst them.

Before her brother sat down he looked at the two of them and gave an approval gesture that made her head spin again.

The conversation started about the logistics of Gregory's plan. As serious as the conversation actually was, armed robbery of government rations was a very serious crime, she and Richard kept glancing at each other as well as whispering occasional jokes. When Richard leaned in to whisper to her, he would lightly touch her shoulder which made her feel electric.

A few rounds in and the planning talks broke down and divulged into casual banter about everyone's lives. The room was full of laughter, not the kind of laughter she was accustomed to hearing at her father's parties where most of the time it was obviously forced, but real genuine laughter. So much laughter that Old Dirge sauntered over and joined the table.

Richard turned to Rhia and asked, "have you ever met Old Dirge?"

Rhia looked at him and replied with friendly sarcasm, "It's my first time here, what do you think?" They both laughed.

Richard asked the guy sitting next to him if he wouldn't mind switching spots with Old Dirge, to which he agreed. Richard waved Old Dirge over to come sit next to him.

"Dirge, this is Rhia. Rhia, this is Dirge."

Old Dirge reached across Richard to shake her hand, "Pleasure to meet you, young lady."

"The pleasure is all mine," Rhia replied with a warm smile on her face. "My Brother has actually told me about you, apparently he got you out of some trouble with some Watchers."

Old Dirge's eyes got wide, "Gregory never mentioned he had a sister, but he damn well saved my ass that night. I imagine you've got a little of his fight in you too, eh?"

She gave a forced humble grin, "I think it must run in the family." Old Dirge looked back and forth at Rhia and Richard before cracking a knowing smile that gave a similar approving look that Gregory had given just a few hours ago.

He got up, bowed and announced, "Nice to meet you young lady, but I do have a kingdom to run." He walked to another table and immediately began to ply his trade in exchange for free drinks. When Richard looked at her after Old Dirge had left their eyes locked, the chemistry was undeniable.

It was such a surreal night. Her brother had almost certainly started something that would make a bigger impact than her night wanderings, she met the rugged looking young man from the alley and he turned out to be someone her brother really liked, and she had laughed more in a night than she had in years. She tried to stay a little cautious, but it looked like change might actually be on the horizon.

Chapter 22

Rhia and Richard sat next to each other at The Rud, while Gregory laid out where the ration caravans would be the most vulnerable to hit. There were several checkpoints on the caravans' way into the richer districts, so they had to catch the trucks between the checkpoints. Both Gregory and Rhia were very familiar with the landscape and knew how to get a few dozen people in position for the ambush without crossing any armed soldiers or police. Rhia had scouted out the times that the trucks which came through in the middle of the night would arrive.

Getting the trucks full of food into their possession was actually the easiest part of the plan because they ran in convoys of four typically with only one armed-guard per truck. With the element of surprise, they should have an easy time overwhelming the guards without firing a shot. They would have a few people blocking the road, which would cause the guards to jump out and try to get them to get out of the way, at that point the rest of Gregory's band would come out of the darkness and tell them to drop their weapons and their radios.

The biggest problem was that they also had to get the trucks back out through the streets without being overtaken, which was a somewhat more difficult proposition. There were places where the trucks could turn off the main highway between checkpoints, but they would only have about 30 minutes to be as far away as possible before someone knew they were gone. Gregory had been having his men scout the side roads, taking meticulous notes on police routes. It would be a narrow route out of there, but one apparently existed. It was a very risky endeavor, but they did have enough people to pull it off.

Richard reached out under the table and squeezed Rhia's hand; she squeezed back. They had seen each other several times since the night of Gregory's rally and every time their chemistry grew. The intensity of the situation, combined with their feelings for each other made them both attracted to one another like moths to a flame.

Whenever he asked her a question, what it was didn't matter, she giggled as she answered. If she asked him a question, he always beamed at her when he answered. There was quite a bit of sexual tension brewing as well. It was about the only thing that they hadn't talked about yet, but they both had it in the back of their minds. Richard had stirred up his courage and knew he was going to ask her to stay with him tonight.

The whole group had noticed It too. If one got to a meeting before the other, when the second one walked through the door and they saw each other–they would both start glowing. It was actually great for group morale to see such a thing as a budding romance when they were talking about extremely dangerous ideas had a way of lighting up the room.

Once the conspirators had gone over the plan several times and everyone started to make casual conversation, Rhia and Richard turned, stared at each other, and locked both hands. There was a long pause. Unlike the night they had first been introduced, it was no longer awkward to sit and stare into each other's eyes.

Richard broke the silence, "I could sit and stare into your eyes forever. They are the most beautiful eyes I've ever seen." His mother's were beautiful, but nothing like the girl staring back at him.

"I've been told similar things before, but never quite like that," Rhia said in response both blushing and batting her eyelashes.

They continued to talk for hours, Richard managing to keep his drinking to a point where he didn't actually get drunk. Rhia smiled at every word Richard said and vice versa. Richard caught enough of the plan that he would be able to do his part, but his mind was only truly focused on one thing. The woman that was there with him. He had never been smitten before in his life. It seemed unreal at first. She was finishing his sentences already. They had only met, officially, a few weeks ago.

"Even Gregory doesn't know about this, but I've been planning future raids in my dorm, would you be interested to come look them over?" Richard asked Rhia. "If you and I work together, I bet Gregory will be blown away."

She smiled and rolled her eyes, "Took you long enough to ask. Of course, I would love to come to your dorm and 'work on your plans'."

Once they got back to his dorm, he flipped on his desk light and it actually turned on. He opened his desk, pulled out a bottle of whiskey, and filled his two glasses. Then, Richard picked up a stack of papers and shuffled them around to where they would be in order. When he turned around to wave her over to the desk, Rhia was standing there in nothing but her bra and underwear. He stood in shock, which just made her laugh.

"There is plenty of time to plan after we pull off the first heist, I'd rather make the most of the evening if it was all the same to you," she said with a wink as she motioned him towards her with a single elegant finger. Richard immediately pulled her towards him, embraced her, caressed her body, and whispered into her ear; "I can't believe how lucky it is I found you."

She put her finger to his lips and whispered back, "for once in your life Richard; don't think, just do." The fire had been lit and the passion was fueled by a deep sense of joy that neither had felt in a long, long while. Richard knew he needed this. Rhia did too.

She downed the glass in one shot without flinching. Richard reached over to do the same, but she grabbed him and tackled him onto his bed. The two entangled themselves and started passionately kissing each other. Item by item she tore off Richard's clothes before taking off the last two pieces of her own. Rhia stopped for a second to throw all of his books on the floor. It didn't bother Richard; they had been all that had loved him for a while — but he had something real now.

She pushed him onto his back and climbed on top of him. It was like nothing Richard had ever experienced before. The way she moved her shapely bronzed body was almost the polar opposite of the way Janice just jaggedly bounced up and down. Instead of just yelling "Yes! Yes! Yes!" over and over, Rhia moaned in a way that told him when he was doing something right.

Eventually she rolled off and pulled him on top of her. He couldn't believe how amazing it felt. She raked her fingernails over his back, sending pleasure throughout his entire body. She grabbed his hands and put them to her throat. He squeezed gently at first, so she put her hands around his and made him squeeze harder which caused her to let out the most beautiful moan he could have ever imagined. They were at it for a few hours and she always kept him guessing. Pure bliss.

When both had finished, they sat in each other's arms staring into each other's eyes. He ran his fingers through her hair. She gently rubbed his back. Eventually she kissed him, got up, poured two more glasses of whiskey, came back, and sat on the side of the bed. He sat up, scooted next to her, and grabbed one. Janice was very attractive, but Rhia was absolutely stunning–both inside and out.

They sat and talked about life, plans for what they would do if their little rebellion worked, both dancing around the fact that they were already falling in love. Richard lit a cigarette and shared it with Rhia.

"Remember that song I said I'd sing for you the first night we actually met," She asked?

Richard thought back to that night, "Yes. The one you are named after. That and a Goddess if I remember correctly." She definitely had lived up to the goddess part.

She hopped into his lap, both of them still undressed, and

she started singing (which, as if he expected any less, was as beautiful as everything else about her); "Rhiannon rings like a bell through the night..." Richard was enraptured by her voice, her presence, and absolutely everything about her. He only managed to hear about half of the words she was singing because his mind was ablaze with thoughts of what life would now be like with her in it. He wished that the moment would last forever.

After she finished the last note, she stood up and found her clothes one by one; "If I don't get back to my father's mansion before he notices I'm gone, you will be down a person for the ambush." She kissed him and said, "I'll see you at the meeting place." Then walked out the door.

Chapter 23

Gregory's plan had been put into action and they were ready. Mark had even joined them. The bulletproof trucks carrying food to the wealthier districts were en route, but Gregory's little band of rebels were waiting and in position. Richard, Mark, and about a dozen others were in an alley to the left of the ambush site. Gregory had a dozen with him on the right side of the alley. Both sides were armed and ready to go. Against both Richard and Gregory's protests, Rhia had insisted that she would be part of the bait team that blocked the road to get the guards out of the trucks.

The trucks rolled up on Rhia's team and stopped. Exactly according to plan, the guards got out of the trucks and approached the bait. The guards yelled at them to disperse, which was the signal. Richard came rushing out brandishing his father's revolver followed closely by everyone from his team, but Mark. Mark had frozen in horror. Thinking about the situation was one thing, but now that he was here it was something else entirely. It didn't matter, the guards turned around to realize they were outgunned four to twelve.

"Put down your guns and your radios," Richard yelled loudly, staring down men holding rifles from 20 feet away.

That was Gregory's signal, he and his team ran up to the trucks and ordered the drivers to get out. Rhia's team was busy tying up the guards who had done as Richard asked. Half of Richard's team doubled back and did the same to the drivers. Two of Gregory's men jumped into each of the trucks and sped off for the turnoff they had mapped out a few hundred yards down the road. With the convoy en route and the eight convoy workers tied up and dragged into a ditch, the rest of them split into smaller groups and scrambled in the direction the convoys would be heading—all taking slightly different routes.

Rhia and Richard grabbed Mark who was still paralyzed in fear and they made their way down a series of alleyways and side streets. They were running as fast as Mark could keep up with. Eventually they made it to a district very close to where the trucks were going to be dropped off. They stopped for a minute to catch their breath, before walking carefully in the dark towards where the trucks had certainly already been dropped. Richard pulled out his pocket watch and saw that their 30 minutes was nearly up.

Richard looked at Mark and smiled, "Don't sweat it man, we pulled it off. You can get in on the next one." Mark didn't look entirely reassured. Richard had grown into himself, but he was still no Gregory. They were only a short way away from the drop site when they heard sirens go off in the distance where the ambush happened. Even Mark wanted to see the trucks in a poor district, so they ran as fast as they could towards it. By the time they got to the four trucks, they saw the rations had already been stripped entirely out of the trucks and nobody else was in sight. All three of them lingered for a moment to savor the success of their plan.

After a little while of savoring the victory, Richard said; "Time to head to The Rud." They took backstreets and alleys the whole way. It was a few mile trek. When they got there, Gregory and more than a dozen of the others were there waiting.

Gregory rushed over to them and hugged Rhia, then Mark, before holding his massive hand out to Richard. As another half dozen of their co-conspirators walked through the door Gregory turned to the three of them and beamed, "We pulled it off. I have a guy in the kitchen listening on the radios we grabbed off of the guards and so far they haven't caught a single one of us. Let's grab a table and celebrate!" Even Mark looked relieved.

Throughout the night, more and more of the little Robin Hood group came trickling in until everyone was accounted for. Drinks flowed and stories were told. Even Old Dirge, who thought they were idiots for doing it, had to congratulate them, joining in on the revelry. Gregory was all over the room congratulating everyone on a job well done. Richard and Rhia sat holding hands just taking in the revelry of it. Eventually Rhia kissed Richard, got up, and said, "I need to talk to my brother for a minute." Richard didn't mind a bit.

Rhia went up to Gregory and waited for him to finish his conversation. When Gregory finally noticed her, he said his congratulations to the group he was talking to one final time and turned to her. She motioned that they should walk to a more secluded part of the bar.

"I've got to tell you something and I'm not sure how you are going to feel about it," she said in a tentative tone.

Gregory's eyes perked up, he donned a half smile, and he sarcastically said, "What on earth could that be, oh wonderful sister of mine?"

"I think I might be in love with Richard."

Gregory let out a loud genuine laugh, "No Shit Sherlock. I knew you two would hit it off. Even before the rally. I'm glad you finally found someone. Mom would've been happy. Dad would lock you in a closet, but what does he know?" They both laughed.

"It just happened. It feels like it was just meant to be. I

don't think either of us could've stopped it if we tried" she said, beaming.

"I feel happy when he's around too, Rhia. I'm happy for both of you. Plus, we both know you would do it anyway regardless of what I thought." She laughed because he was right.

Gregory paused for a moment, "We're doing it, Rhia, we're actually doing it. I couldn't be happier. The time has come to see some real justice in the world."

Chapter 24

Mark knew Richard could handle whatever job he was given to help in the takeover of the food caravans. He had known ever since he met Richard that Richard could do anything if he put his mind to it. He's seen him do it time and time again. He remembered when he first met Richard. Richard was hung over and hadn't studied for his understanding spreadsheets exam. Mark asked how Richard was going to pass if he didn't study. Richard simply said, "I'll figure it out. I always do. You'll see." Sure enough, Richard did pass the exam, but just barely. He showed Mark his exam score. The professor had written on the paper "I can tell that you aren't trying. 39/50." Richard was much less outwardly cynical back then. His noticeable brooding started right about the time they switched to easier assignments that you either got a green check mark or a red X.

That seemed like a lifetime ago to Mark. He didn't know that he'd be able to do his part in Gregory's ambitious plan. He felt overwhelmed. His fingernails were bleeding from his biting them to the nub every night. But, he made a promise to his friends and he was going to follow through with it.

Mark wasn't even sure why he had a gun, he didn't know if he could use it. Richard had given him some tips, but Richard wasn't exactly trained himself. Gregory had found a suitable soundproof place for people to practice shooting as any kind of gunfire would alert the authorities. Mark did get comfortable enough holding it, but, pulling it if someone was firing at him, that was a different story.

As they walked to the meeting point, Mark watched Richard in awe. The way he handled himself in a moment of crisis seemed so natural, and so deliberate. He tucked his gun in the holster like he's done it millions of times before. The rosewood revolver fit perfectly in Richard's hand, and Mark knew that if Richard had to fire it, Richard would have no hesitation before releasing the boom. Mark told himself he'd be like that someday, if he just kept watching Richard he'd learn.

The ambush went perfectly, even though he did freeze up when it came time to actually rush out and point his gun at the guards. They were stealthy, efficient, and left just as quickly as they all arrived. The four trucks had enough food to feed hundreds of people for weeks. It seemed like a dream to Mark. He'd never felt that kind of danger and excitement followed by joy before in his life.

Mark looked at Rhia. He barely knew her, but he could tell she saw the same thing in Richard that he did. Richard might not be Gregory when it came to inspirational speeches, but Richard did have a way about himself. Mark noticed the way she twirled her hair in her fingers when she was around him, the way she laughed at the things he said, and the way she always seemed to be facing him no matter where they were. Mark could feel the sparks too, but then again, so could everyone else.

It was that kind of attraction he saw first-hand that gave him some extra motivation to do what he had agreed upon. He thought maybe if he learned to be brave, that he'd find his own Rhia. That not only would he be helping a worthy cause, he'd also discover a woman who had that same passion as Richard and Rhia's. There were actually many other girls that had taken part in the heist, Gregory didn't care who you were as long as you were willing to fight for what is right. Mark didn't dare tell anyone (not even Richard), but, deep down, it was all he could think about. He would find his Rhia. He knew he would.

Mark was happy he was in the team with Richard and Rhia. After they had the trucks secured and everyone was scattering, he still stood frozen until they pulled him out of it. His fear immediately turned into adrenaline and he ran as fast and far as he ever had, keeping up with his taller, more athletic, companions.

Eventually they all stopped to catch their breath. Richard apparently sensed he was still nervous, "Mark, my friend. We did it. *You* did it. You're not going to regret this. You're stronger than you know. We're building something big. You're my trusty right-hand man. Don't fret. This is part of a new reality we're carving out together."

"Thanks Richard. I, um, I'm not sure how to respond. You're doing much more than I am, but I appreciate the words. I can feel this electricity and it excites me, I want to be around it all the time. There's something happening that I've never felt. Before I met you, I'd usually be sleeping or reading some trashy sci-fi book at this time of night. I wouldn't have come this far with you if I didn't believe."

"I know," Richard said before joyfully adding, "Those Shit Brains were caught with their pants down. We are taking the power back. You've got the power. More than you know. Just being a part of this gives us all power. We're giving power back to the people. It's exciting, don't you think?"

"I don't know how much power I have, Richard, but I am excited. I'm excited to see people lifted up and the powers-that-be knocked down a peg or two. I never dreamed we could do it like this. It seemed too easy, but you all are smart. You have it all figured out. I actually believe that we can succeed "

"I agree, my friend. We're on the right path. It's going to get even better, I promise!"

Richard looked at his pocket watch, "We've got about three minutes before they realize the trucks were stolen. I know we are all supposed to meet at The Rud, but I would like to see if the trucks got to their destination." He looked at Rhia who nodded her agreement. "We aren't that far away, let's walk quietly and keep our eyes out for trouble." Sirens went off at the ambush site, which made Mark's heart start to race. He kept that to himself and followed his friends.

When they got to the trucks, they were entirely empty. In less than half an hour the starving masses had grabbed the rations out of 4 entire trucks. The job was complete, so they headed to *The Rud* to see how the others had fared.

Mark was excited to see that Gregory had made it along with about a dozen others. Gregory even gave Mark a hug when he saw him and reassured Mark, Rhia, and Richard that nobody had been caught yet. They sat down and started drinking and it wasn't long before Mark's fear turned to pride. He couldn't help but keep thinking about the way Richard had spoken assertively with a rifle pointed directly at him. Mark would be brave like that one day, he just knew it.

Chapter 25

As Rhia sat in The Rud celebrating with her brother, Richard, and the others she was absolutely thrilled. The heist had gone off beautifully. None of them had slept very much in the last several days, but she felt more awake and alive than she had ever been.

The crew had expected it to go well, but not *this* well. Richard had been the most worried about what might happen, but Rhia felt that he was worried about *her*, and not the mission itself. Even if he knew she'd be just fine. She had been in situations much more dangerous than this at least ten times in the last six months alone. But, she felt flattered all the same that Richard showed his concern for her safety, regardless.

She sat there and watched Richard as he talked, laughed,

and joked with his friends in an unreserved animated way that was genuine and endearing. He had masked his insecurities with wittiness the first night they had met (and at times many nights after), but as the weeks had gone on, he had become more and more sure of himself and who he was quickly becoming. The natural handsomeness, that was still noticeable in spite of the disheveled appearance of the young man the night that she had mistakenly knocked him to the pavement, was no longer something you had to look closely to see.

For being someone with clear demons, Richard still acted like such a gentleman. Not the buttoned-up kind of gentleman that had been paraded in front of her before, but the kind that you could rely on for anything. He cared more about what she thought than how she looked and was noticeably infatuated whenever she would speak intelligently about the many things Richard liked to talk about. She knew that the others in their group benefitted from the company of the rest, but the way that she and Richard inspired each other to be better was an incredible thing to be part of.

Their first time they had slept together had left an impression on Rhia too. He held her in a way she hadn't ever been held before. He asked her what she wanted him to do, and he did it. They made love–and it felt like the rest of the world did not exist. She wanted to feel that again. The feeling was elevated a thousand times by the high of the heist.

They drank and strategized at the bar, as they had done before after Gregory's speech, but this time it felt different. As they drank, Rhia noticed Richard looking at her every chance he got, even when he left to congratulate others in the group. He winked at her. She winked back. It was as if they were the only two people in the crowded room.

Whereas Richard asked Rhia if she'd like to go up to his place the first time, this time Rhia led the way, although she made it sound like it was his idea.

"Richard, it's been a long day. Yet, I don't feel tired at all. Do you?" Rhia asked purposefully.

"Not in the slightest. This day will be one we're going to remember for a long time and I mean that. I'm not even that drunk. I mean, I'm drunk, but I'm more happy than wasted." He replied, OBVIOUSLY MISSING THE POINT.

Rhia laughed and touched his arm with her fingertip. "Oh, Richard, you can be so smart and so dumb at the same time. What do you think we should do next?" she asked, with a coy look on her face.

"We take more ration trucks. Like, *a lot more* trucks. Take the whole damn system back from them, we take what we have here and we expand. We get more food and help more people..." He trailed off as her expression went from coy to condescending. It occurred to him that the alcohol and excitement had him blabbering on in the wrong direction.

"Well, obviously," Rhia said before giving Richard a look and biting her bottom lip for just a second. "I mean tonight. Are we going to stay here and keep celebrating? Or what do you have in mind?"

It was at that moment that the lightbulb in Richard's head went off as to exactly what she was saying.

"I was thinking we could maybe leave and you and I could celebrate alone," he said, rubbing his chin and grabbing his collar, before Rhia took out her hand and grabbed his shirt sleeve with her fingertips.

"I was thinking the same thing. How did you know?" she whispered into his ear.

"Oh, I have my ways," he said, with a wink.

Rhia led Richard up to the doorway just outside his dorm. She grabbed the key out of his pocket and opened it. Before they entered, she grabbed the cigarette out of Richard's mouth and laughed.

"You know these will kill you," she said, only half joking with him. "You should really think about quitting."

"Well, if it's not one thing, it's another," Richard responded.

"Yeah, I suppose so," Rhia said in a non-judgmental defiant response. "This night has been so great, hasn't it? I wish I could take a picture. I'd keep it forever."

"Me too, Rhia. We did something," Richard said in a somber tone he hadn't had in the bar.

The two sat in Richard's dorm. They chatted briefly. The feeling between them was much more intense even than last time. A bomb could have dropped just outside the dorm, and neither of them would have noticed.

Once inside his room, Richard began kissing Rhia and squeezed her tightly around the waist. Rhia took off Richard's shirt and unbuckled his pants. She grabbed his hand and let him unbutton her shirt and bra. She moaned in agreement. She had felt pleasure before, but never the pleasure of a robin hood figure she had twice chanced into before meeting and committing armed robbery with. Despite the occasional bite, she was a gentle lover. The lovemaking lasted all night and into the morning. They slept a little, then would go back again for another round. They'd do it again, only in a different position. Rhia felt Richard scratch her back. She scratched his back in the mark of love's passionate embrace. Whatever the nights ahead would bring, she was with the

187

best man she had ever slept with before.

Rhia's father had become very busy lately–authorities in the city were obsessed with the little band of rebels growing in the city and he (never in a million years imagining his daughter to be amongst them) was so preoccupied with readying the men under his command for a response that he had stopped bothering to check if she was around. She was free to spend her time as she wanted to. As the morning turned into afternoon, the two were still lying in bed together. Rhia finally got up and grabbed some whiskey out of his desk. She grabbed his two glasses and filled them nearly full. Richard, who was just waking up himself, laughed.

"At least someone can read my mind, but isn't it kind of early for you?" he laughed. He was already a seasoned veteran at day drinking, but wasn't sure if she would appreciate that about him.

"Early? It's afternoon!" Rhia responded. "Plus, we have to get up and do *something.* We've got the next heist to get ready for, but we have a few hours to kill."

"Right, Second round. Gregory isn't wasting time, is he? Strike the iron while it's hot and whatnot." Richard stretched before grabbing a cigarette out of a pack in his pants and lighting it.

"My brother is very ambitious," she said casually, "there will always be another mission. He is the type of person who won't be satisfied until the whole broken system comes tumbling down...and even then, he probably won't quit. He is just like that."

She stopped to look at Richard sitting on the side of his bed, mostly naked and casually smoking a cigarette like he was perfectly content with the world at that moment. He had made an effort to trim his facial hair since the night she first crashed into him in an alley in the middle of the night. The angst and cynicism he wore on his sleeve the night they had spoken after Gregory's speech had given way in the weeks since to a profound individual growing into his own shoes. He wasn't ever going to have the kind of magnetism that pulled people in the way that her brother did, but he had grown more confident. She preferred the sharp edges of his personality over her brother's, at times, overly calculated political-esque persona.

Rhia handed a glass to Richard and joked, "We obviously shouldn't be drunk tonight, but a few to pass the time wouldn't hurt. We can sit here and drink to a sun that you can hardly see."

"Yes, yes we can." Richard said, grabbing the glass. He leaned over and gave her a kiss before downing half of the cheap whiskey in a single drink.

"To us and whatever will come, will come" Rhia said.

"C'est La Vie" Richard said, in an obvious attempt to impress her. He stared out the window at the dull sun for a moment before reflecting, "It's pretty incredible to be a part of something that is changing things in, at least, some small way. I can't help but worry for us." She had donned an indignant look that clearly said, 'I can worry about myself' so he quickly added; "All of us. Yes, you and I–but also Mark and Gregory and everybody. I don't understand this world the way that your brother does, but I know enough to know that the system won't go down quietly." His familiar brooding streak flared up.

Rhia wasn't without worry. She too knew as well as anyone that the world was full of the type of people like her father's party guests and that they had her father and the army that he served at their disposal. But she also knew their cause was just and didn't want to waste a few precious hours of peace worrying about what could happen. She leaned over to his ear and whispered, "Don't you worry, we know exactly what we're doing," before kissing him on the cheek. She playfully reached over, grabbed his hand with the drink in it, brought it to her mouth and took a swig out of his before taking a sip of hers as well.

The two of them sat and stared into each other's eyes. Richard in love with the fiery brilliant girl who had not let the decay on the world around her dim the stars in her eyes: Rhia in love with a handsome young man who defied convention and wore his wits more comfortably than the boys who had been paraded in front of her had worn their fancy clothes. By choice, danger was on the horizon for both of them for at least the foreseeable future–but both were content to be at peace, there with each other, even if it was just for an afternoon.

Chapter 26

Gregory, Richard, Mark, Rhia, and some of the core group of their little band of would-be rebels (Old Dirge had begun calling them Gregory's band of merry men and women) gathered around a table at The Rud killing time before the raid they had planned for the evening. Excitement and nerves for their second ambush were high, so they sat discussing the details of their plan, even though they had gone over it countless times before. Richard slowly sipped a beer. He and Rhia had stopped drinking a few hours ago, but the stakes of armed robbery had him thirsty again.

When it became abundantly clear that they were going in circles, talking just to talk, and that everyone there knew every inch of the plan from front to back–Gregory stood up in a display of finality and spoke; "We all know what needs to be done. It will be just like last time. The only difference is more trucks and more food. We aren't doing ourselves any favors by beating the dead horse. The sun is setting and it wouldn't hurt to get to the meeting place before the rest of the group do." The lot of them followed Gregory's lead, gathered themselves, and left towards the ambush site.

The core group made casual conversation as they walked further towards their destination while the sky darkened around them. All of them were so focused on the mission at hand that nobody (including Mark) even bothered to think about how they would look if they were spotted by Citizen Watchers. Watchers wouldn't harass a group of a dozen or so people at first sight, but they could make plenty of trouble if they got a good description of any of the people amongst Gregory's little band. Sometimes through luck, bravado goes unnoticed–and they made it to the spot where they were meeting the others without incident.

Some of Gregory's military friends had stashed the guns they were going to use nearby. The vanguard group retrieved them and readied them to be handed out. Richard had no need to borrow one of Gregory's arms because he favored his father's revolver. It tucked easily away in the waistband of his worn-out denim jeans and he felt poetic vengeance knowing he was using something of his father's to help take down the system that had taken his father away.

Others began to arrive and soon the time came to move into place to await the trucks they were about to seize.

The convoy arrived right on time. Gregory was pretty sure that they wouldn't fall for bait by stopping to disperse people in the road a second time, so they had to take them as they were stopped at the checkpoint where some of the drivers would get out of the vehicles to register with the guards at a checkpoint. Pairs of people had been assigned to get in the trucks as fast as possible and drive off the second they had the guards and drivers at the checkpoint under control, the rest of them were tasked with overwhelming the dozen or so guards that would be there–hopefully into surrendering before any shooting was necessary.

Lights at the compound were enough to see some of the drivers exiting their trucks. Gregory ordered them to move in.

All of the planning and endless hours of conversation launched into motion in a split second as the group boldly rushed out of the cover of darkness to swarm the checkpoint. Exactly as planned, the group caught the convoy by surprise and the guards laid down their weapons without a fight. Gregory and one of his military looking friends were the first to get into one of the trucks and start to drive away. A few seconds later, Richard and a second one of Gregory's military friends hopped in another and followed Gregory. Rhia and a third followed Richard. Mark and a fourth were behind her. Soon all of the other trucks were in their control and en route to be dropped in a poor district for people to come and raid. Everyone had done it in lock step, like clockwork.

It was already pretty late when they arrived where they had planned to drop the food. As the trucks rolled to a stop one by one, they opened up the backs for anyone to come feast. The group were excited to find the trucks almost overflowing with food. Gregory pulled out a bell that would be heard for many blocks (Old Dirge suggested ringing a bell as a signal for people of the poor district to come get food one of the times he listened in on the planning; Dirge thought they were all out of their minds for doing what they were doing, but was quick to offer advice on how to commit armed robbery with style and flair). The cabal of volunteers accompanying the supply caravan took off. Some of them grabbed a box or two of food for themselves. The deed was done and the trucks would be found by the authorities in the morning, empty-just like the first time.

In the middle of the synchronized operation Mark had said to Richard that he had never seen something so meticulously planned out done so well in spite of all the different moving parts.

"Richard, you guys have thought of almost everything here, haven't you?" Mark said.

"That's the idea. You don't operate with a machete. You get a scalpel. We've got a good thing going here. Now we just can't get too cocky," Richard brooded.

"You? Cocky! Nah," Rhia said sarcastically after exiting the back of the truck. "It's a shame we can't keep a fleet of these. Bullet proof vehicles would come in handy in a pinch."

"I mean, that would be quite the power move. I suppose if we had enough people and guns, we could pull them into a district and set up a stronghold...," Richard trailed off because the idea of setting up an armed garrison where the authorities could find them went well beyond the scope of the Robin Hood hit and run operation they were running now.

"But, we're doing this to help the people-which we are. This night has gone better than the last. I'm optimistic that there is a new era on the horizon. If we traveled in stolen trucks, it would be a bloodbath" Richard said solemnly.

"Yeah, but it would be one hell of a fight," Rhia laughed before trailing off for a second. She too understood the enormity of an armed conflict. She had heard enough stories from her father to know that (even for the best of causes) war was never a good thing, especially for those who fought it.

"I'm glad my brother has kept up a resistance. We're taking the corrupt system down a convoy at a time. They're not going to like seeing another big group of trucks emptied out without any idea of where it all went," Rhia said, with the stars absolutely shining in her eyes. There was beauty and danger in equal measure and Richard could think of nothing more magnificent.

"They won't. We can't get cocky though. The second we let our guard down is the moment they pounce. If my years of having the systems' slogans shoved down my throat at school have taught me anything, it is that the powers to be are not going to be happy having their absolute control challenged. We're not done yet, but it does feel like we are delivering justice. Those Shit Brains had no idea it was coming either time. Still, change always comes at a price and sometimes one you never want to pay," Richard said, with the thought of his father being taken away in the back of his mind. He knew it was more difficult than they were making it out to be.

Still, it felt so good to see people living in the area starting to materialize out of the night and rush to the trucks that Mark and Richard hugged and gave a congratulatory whoop and holler. Richard's mind knew that they were playing a dangerous game, but in that moment his heart felt like they could do anything. They had tasted victory twice and nobody could deny that they were the ones making it all happen. Word would spread amongst the common people starving in the decay and squalor that this world had become and the movement would continue to grow. It had been way too long since anything good had happened in the city.

After the food was delivered by Gregory's little band and the quickly emptying trucks were out of sight in the distance; Mark,

Gregory, Richard, Rhia, and many of the others made for The Rud to again toast to beating the system and spend the wee hours of the night in revelry.

Chapter 27

Old Dirge joined the group at The Rud. Richard, Rhia, Gregory and Mark were again in high spirits after a second successful mission. Dirge ordered a round of shots on Richard's tab and asked what it felt like when they saw the faces of the guards who were outmatched and outgunned. It was something Gregory had been dying to describe to Old Dirge since the first raid because he was eager to give Dirge another wild tale to spin in his never-ending quest for free drinks. He began before they arrived at the checkpoint.

Gregory flashed his natural charisma, "Luck was on our side, we had a clear night. The moonlight gave off just enough light so that we could see without the need for any lights that might have given us away. It's been long enough since anyone has put up any kind of coordinated fight, that the men guarding the food caravans were never going to see it coming. Between their lack of readiness and the cover of darkness, it was like taking candy from a baby." He picked up one of the shots Dirge had ordered and paused long enough to toast the others before continuing, "The caravan guards aren't as cruel as the Citizen's Watch, but that is a pretty low bar. You can bet that none of them would bat an eye at firing into a hungry crowd. Cowardly submission to a bad thing has every bit the impact as those who embrace it with malice.

It was apparent when we got the jump on them just how cowardly they were. Like any would-be bully taking comfort in their status and numbers, when the tables turned and they were caught outnumbered with their pants around their ankles–they squealed like the cornered pigs they are. They were so happy to leave with their sad lives, they couldn't hand over the trucks fast enough. It's always a welcome sight to see dumb fear on the faces of those who would lord themselves above the rest, but *you* know that as well as anyone Dirge."

"I would've loved to have seen it," said Dirge, clearly reveling in the thought. "These old legs don't move like they used to, but I do love to see some assholes shit themselves."

Dirge laughed his joking laugh that endeared his way onto many another man's bar-tab before musing, "I'd almost be willing to drag my walking corpse along just for that sight alone!" Something about his joking aura was underwritten by genuine admiration and his words edged on an honest offer.

Gregory jumped at the opening, "We could *always* use you out there. You might think you're too old and everyone might think you are just a drunk, but that isn't a complete deal breaker. Your bones may be old, but your balls are made of steel–which is exactly the kind of crazy we need."

Greg laughed and patted Dirge on the back before turning to speak to the others, "And more to the point, this fight belongs to everybody. Old or young, drunk or sober, poor or rich, it doesn't matter. The blight on our society is shared by all. Nobody's hands are clean, but everybody can do their part."

"If it's as easy as you all keep saying, I just might. God Damn, I just might!"

Gregory looked Old Dirge in the eye and voiced so the whole bar could hear, "Just remember, we're not going in 'guns-a-blazing. We're taking the food, not shooting people up."

Gregory put back another of the shots and his voice got louder, "We rob the corrupt. That's the key. We're taking what they would give to those who have too much already and giving it to those who need it. The next one is going to be massive; we are taking an entire city's worth of rations. If you come with us, you have a chance to make history. It will be the start of something bigger, won't it Richard?"

Richard was caught a little off guard that Gregory would bring him into the center of attention as Gregory had a poise and a skill of persuasion that he himself did not possess, but he could feel pride swelling up and took his chance in the moment.

"It's going to shake things up" said Richard, in a knowing and collected manner that he had only recently started working on. "It will be profound for us and the people we will feed," Richard said, flashing his best approximation of a charismatic grin. Emboldened by the atmosphere, he continued with more zeal; "Everything we've done up until now has led up to it. The world we want to see won't come overnight, but this is the kind of thing that will get the kind of attention that change needs to grow. More than making history, we have the chance to do what is right." He grabbed two of the remaining shots off the table and downed them to cheers from the room.

As the onlooking crowd turned their attention back to their own individual revelry, Richard turned his attention to Rhia. She was beaming at him, with her eyes shining brighter than he had ever seen them. In that moment he felt the stirrings of pride because he immediately recognized that the way she was now looking at him was exactly how his mother had looked at his father whenever his father had spoken in front of people for the first many years of

Richard's life. He would never get the chance to know for sure, but in that moment he absolutely believed that his father would have been proud of him.

Even though the people filling the bar were broken off into smaller groups celebrating amongst themselves, Richard's table was still squarely the center of attention. This was made amply clear when, allowing himself to be caught up in the moment, Richard pulled Rhia towards him into a passionate kiss–which received applause as well as 'ooos' and whistles from around them. Both Richard and Rhia were too happy in the moment to blush at the attention. They were not the only ones overjoyed either, all throughout the bar there was a palpable feeling that everyone there was a part of something bigger.

Richard, Rhia, Mark, Gregory, and Old Dirge sat at the table that was the center of everyone's attention and enjoyed each other's company well into the night. Spirits were high and they felt confident that they were really doing something that could make the world a better place. The whole bar was there to celebrate with them because everyone in it knew that what they were doing was right. This would be a turning point that was going to change everything and they drank comfortably in that knowledge.

Chapter 28

Gregory's band of armed merry men and women huddled down a dark side street waiting for the time to come to launch the ambush. There was no moon to light the night sky and a fog hung in the air. Mark, Richard, Old Dirge, Gregory, and Rhia handed out flashlights equipped with low red lights. Unlike last time, when there had been enough moonlight to safely navigate, they would have to light their own way.

They may have risked attempting to take the trucks in the cover of complete darkness, but it had rained recently and the deep puddles in the potholes of the side streets on the way to the ambush were enough to grab an ankle-the sound of splashing water as someone freed themselves could be enough to alert someone to their location. To reduce the chances of lights giving away their approach anyway, Gregory had insisted that they use the low red lights he had installed in their flashlights that could only be seen from a short distance as long as they were only pointed at the ground. The plan was for them to shut the lights off when the band of rebels were in sight of the light from the compound guarding the checkpoint.

Gergory had also gotten a hold of flares to light a distance away from the ambush to distract the guards from the outpost and hopefully draw some of them out into the night. It was just one more thing to gain more of an edge, but was likely overkill. Everything would be fine if they kept to the plan.

They planned on taking a city's worth of rations, but with the additional crew they picked up through word-of-mouth (as their previous successes were quickly becoming urban legends), it would be just as doable. Even though there were many more trucks in this convoy than either of their last two robberies, they had more than enough people to handle them. Most would have four of Gregory's men to them as they sped off, twice as many as they had used previously.

Gregory had meticulously timed the operation out. He planned exactly where they would approach the trucks to allow the band of would-be rebels enough time to drive them off through the alleyways with precision. The exact amount of time the Trucks stopped at the checkpoint to be catalogued was consistent every time his men had scouted the convoy. Gregory even had a part of his team dedicated to destroying the radios and phones of the checkpoint as the rest of them sped off with the food.

It was all set up to succeed again. They had everything in place.

Before they took off for the checkpoint, Mark sat next to Richard and fiddled his flashlight on and off again and again as he attempted to calm his nerves. Richard, who was also on edge, grabbed the flashlight in Mark's hands and turned to his friend.

"You might be nervous, but please don't give away our position by accidentally blinking out some message. Don't be nervous. We've got this. We planned for what to do if the weather worsened. Nothing major has changed." Richard said, more to reassure himself than Mark.

"I know. It's going to go fine. It is. But, what if it doesn't? Have you considered that?" Mark responded.

Richard *had* thought of that, but knew very well that dwelling on what could go wrong wouldn't help them now. "I can't stop to think about that," Richard said, in a tone that attempted to convey both sympathy and certainty. Practicing his newfound confidence when speaking about their cause, he continued, "We have to think that this will work and that there is no other possibility. That there is no chance that this doesn't work. You're thinking too much, Mark-and you as much as anyone can believe me when I say overthinking things isn't always a good thing. As long as we all step up and do our jobs, you've got nothing to worry about. Have I been wrong about these raids yet?"

"Well, uh, no. I guess, I guess you haven't," Mark agreed.

"You know as well as I do that what we are doing is right. We have a plan and we have way more people than the last two times. I know you are capable of more than you think you are. You are an incredible guy, you know that right?" Richard clapped Mark on the back and repeated, "You know that right?"

"Right!" Mark called out, catching on to the mini pep-talk that Richard was giving.

"Right. So just trust the plan and do your part. We are absolutely capable of this. I know you have this in you," Richard had been getting better at sounding inspirational and the reassurance of his tone was a level of convincing that Mark had only heard from Gregory.

Mark felt legitimate confidence and answered back, "Got it, my friend! Thank you. You're right. This is gonna go well."

"Mark. You know I love you. We're almost there. You're gonna become a man, Mark." Undercutting the mini-speech with a joke, Richard nudged Mark's ribs and winked at him; "Maybe you'll even finally get some chest hair on you."

"Ha, ha. Very funny. But thank you, Richard. That means a lot." Mark looked relaxed for the first time.

"Of course. You're my best friend in the world. We're taking down the Shit Brains a big peg here and it sure has been a long time coming," Richard said while lighting up a cigarette.

Rhia let out a fake cough.

Richard looked at her and said with a more somber tone than he had used with Mark, "They have guns too, I'm going to enjoy a cigarette even if it is my last. Also, I love you. I hope I can say it a million more times, but we are going up against a lot of guns."

She grabbed the cigarette out of his mouth, threw it to the ground, and stared him straight in the face for a moment. "I love you too, I hope I can say it a million more times as well."

They started the short approach to the spot Gregory had picked for the ambush. This time they were hitting a very large convoy as it was stopped at a checkpoint, but more trucks meant more guards with guns. It was riskier, but the amount of food they were planning on seizing this time made it worth it. The size of the convoy limited their ability to maneuver through the city and the best route to where they were planning on dropping them forked directly from the Checkpoint.

With the darkness of the night near pitch black, they could

approach more openly and with larger numbers without needing to worry about being exposed. A convoy of nearly twenty ration trucks were visible in the lights from the checkpoint's compound, parked and waiting to cross. Gregory gave the word and they began the approach with their dim red flashlights. He and Old Dirge split off with a large group so they could ambush the waiting trucks from both sides.

Mark, Richard, and Rhia approached the convoy in a group of nearly three dozen of Gregory's armed troops and waited just outside of the light cast by the checkpoint for the other group to get in place. Gregory and Dirge approached from the other direction with slightly more people following them. On top of the darkness, the whole scene was further blurred by dense fog. They watched as Gregory's team lit the flares a distance away and threw them out into the night. The flares lit up the night, a ways away from the checkpoint, but no alarms sounded and no guards rushed out to investigate. Unwavering, Gregory ordered his men forward.

From across the road, Richard saw Gregory's men moving into the faint light. He ordered his group to advance and the two teams converged. Then all hell broke loose. As the band of would be rebels approached, the backs of the trucks in the convoy opened up and soldiers poured out.

Gregory was the first to raise the alarm; "Holy shit. We've got a big fucking problem. They're armed. They're outside the trucks. They're waiting for us. Retreat. I repeat, get the fuck out of here. Now, now, now."

The soldiers opened fire. Many of the ambushers ignored Gregory's orders and fired back, but any advantage they might have had disintegrated into a haze of gunpowder. An alarm had gone off. Spotlights came up. The teams began to run opposite ways to safety. More were being shot. Rhia ducked as she could hear bullets flying past her ears.

Mark took off a few yards behind Richard. He held his gun tight. The last thing he wanted to do was drop it and get shot while he was picking it up. They had made it almost into the cover of darkness, mere yards from disappearing safely into the distance. With only a short distance left to run, out of the corner of his eye, he saw a woman kneeling. She had been shot.

The soldiers had taken losses too, but were quickly forming into smaller groups to pursue the remaining rebels back through the streets. Mark had a decision to make, because they would start their advance at any moment. Either continue to flee, or protect the woman. On any other day, Mark would've fled. He would've lived to regret it, but he would've been alive. However, as he heard this woman scream, he knew what he had to do.

"Hey Richard! I gotta turn around. Cover me!" He screamed.

Richard heard him and looked back. "Don't do it. Mark, don't..." But, it was too late. Running back into the fray through bullets spraying through the fog from the direction of the convoy, Mark got close to the woman and grabbed her hand. "You're safe now. I'm going to protect you," he said. "Just hang tight. We're going to get you out of here." Just then four camo-laden soldiers in pursuit appeared out of the fog in front of them. Mark raised his rifle.

"Fuck you!" he screamed as he pulled the trigger with his eyes trained on them. His gun fired in all directions toward the men. Three of them went down, one last man remained standing. Mark had to reload.

The last remaining soldier trained his rifle at the woman. While Mark was reloading, he yelled out, "Shit Brains. You can't take me!"

The guard fired three rounds into the woman, killing her instantly. Richard, who had run through the fog after Mark, first saw the dead guards lying in front of Mark. Then he saw the woman laying lifeless next to Mark. Mark had smoke coming from his rifle. The guard trained his rifle on Mark. Richard let out a scream, but it was too late. Now both Mark and the woman were filled with bullet holes. Richard pulled out his father's revolver and shot all six rounds into the man who had just killed his best friend.

Richard dropped to his knees. He couldn't believe what he just saw. Why did Mark go back? How did he miss the last guard? Where was Gregory? Why couldn't Richard have gotten there just a few seconds sooner? It was all too much for him, but Rhia tugged at him to stand up as more guards began yelling to advance off in the distance.

"Come on. We have to get out of here *now*! There's more coming!" she warned him.

"I, I can't just leave Mark. I can't leave him..." The tears in Richard's eyes were pouring down.

"Richard, there's no time for this. I'm sorry...you know I am, but we need to get out of here *now*!" Richard snapped into reality and allowed her to whisk him to safety. They made it a decent way away from where the firefight had taken place and found that Gregory was already waiting for them with less than twenty left of the original group. Richard and Rhia were two of the last to escape the shooting gallery. As the last few stragglers stumbled out of the fog, Gregory's face wore a look of stern stoic defeat. Only his eyes betrayed the sorrow that he felt at having lost so many of his friends.

Gregory's sad eyes flashed with relief when he saw his sister and Richard emerge from the darkness and fog, but fell knowingly when he didn't see Mark trailing right behind them. As Richard and Rhia got closer, he could see a hallowed look on his sister's face that she had never worn before and tears streaming down Richard's face. He immediately ran towards them, steeling his nerve to be brave for his friend and sister. Once he reached Richard and Rhia, he actually found himself at a loss for words.

Richard looked at Gregory through blurry eyes and blurted out, "I'll explain later. I'm not sure what he was thinking. He just yelled he had to go back. I saw a woman there. She was kneeling. He did his best, Gregory. He almost made it. If only I had gone back a few seconds sooner. I, it's, it's my fault. I'm sorry. I let it happen." Richard was choking on his tears.

Gregory grabbed Richard by both shoulders with his massive hands, "There is no time for that now. We all fucked up, Richard. You're going to make yourself sick, or worse-join him. Let's get back to safety. We're not doing any good standing here waiting for the firing line."

After the battle, they estimated that more than half of their crew had been killed or taken prisoner. Some in the crew were quick to point out that they had taken out a good number of the guards too. The food, however, was lost to them. The trucks went through the checkpoint. Any way they looked at it, they had failed. Mark dying was the cherry on top. Suddenly, their plan looked foolish. They had been outmanned and outgunned. Nobody knew what to do next.

Old Dirge stood up and said something that was more profound and inspirational than anything Richard had ever heard him say before; "They'll remember us. Those fuckers. We're famous now, gents. Get used to it. We're on the tips of all their tongues. Get ready for more." They weren't ready, though. It wasn't supposed to go like this.

Chapter 29

Mark and Richard were walking to the meeting point for their latest incursion. Mark felt like he wasn't doing enough to justify him continuing to go on the heists. He had always been a worrier and lately he had been doing things he never in a million years thought he would. The thought of what his Gran would say if she was still around and knew what he was up to. She had always raised him to be cautious and not make any commotion. He had definitely been doing the opposite lately and her voice was always in the back of his head.

Even a year ago, Mark would not have recognized the person he had grown into. So much had happened. First it was just him and Richard adventuring to bars, which was already out of character compared to his previous life. Now, it was full blown armed robbery in the name of a revolution. As the two of them walked, his anxiety grew. Finally, he stopped walking. It took Richard a few steps to notice. When he did, Richard doubled back and stood looking at Mark with a puzzled expression.

Mark fumbled for words for a few seconds before blurting out, "Honestly Richard, what am I doing here? I just hold a gun and stand around scared. Other people rush right in and point it at the guards. I've gotten on a truck. I've escaped with the rest of you. That's all I'm doing. I actually think I might stay home this time, if that's ok with you,"

Richard's face grew serious and showed a spark of the inner leader that Mark had seen him starting to become. Mark could see him collect his thoughts before replying.

With a calm and inspirational tone that Mark had only recently begun to see, Richard spoke; "I'm sorry my friend, but it's not ok. Sure, you haven't been in the thick of things yet. So what? By my reckoning, you've still done more than most people ever would. I've even talked to several people after our raids. You help in ways others don't. I was talking to one of the guys after our last raid. Al, the former plumber. He was telling me how much your conversations have meant to him. Since his business dried up and his wife passed he hasn't had much to live for. He told me he had all but given up on the world.

He went on for a good while about how you helped him. He said he hasn't talked much about his wife passing until he met you. And look, he's not the only one. There are others who have said you've helped them calm their nerves because if you can tough it out, so can they. We need you, Mark. It's as simple as that. When I asked you to come along with me through this, I did it for a reason. Not just because you're my friend, but because you show courage and you bring out the best in people."

Mark's usual skittishness melted. Something deep down inside Mark was moved by how his friend spoke. It was eerie how much Richard had grown since meeting Gregory and Rhia. His once brooding friend was now calm yet assertive. The change made Mark happy for his friend and the confidence Richard was showing had definitely caught ahold of him. Mark just nodded and the two started off again.

They walked to the meeting area, where Rhia was already waiting for them. She ran up and kissed Richard before turning to hug Mark.

"How are you two feeling tonight?" Rhia asked.

Both Mark and Richard were silent for a moment before exchanging looks. Mark's reservations were fairly well in check, but Richard was giving him a 'do I tell her' look. They had all become so close lately that Mark gave his friend the 'go ahead' shrug.

Turning back to Rhia, Richard said; "Well. Mark is a little worried that he isn't being a valuable member of our little band of Rebels."

Rhia turned to Mark and donned a look of sympathy and encouragement, "You know that isn't true, right?"

Mark looked down at his feet for a second before replying, "I mean, it's probably just jitters. I wasn't exactly born brave like you and Gregory and Richard. Every time we're out doing this, I can't help but think about what my Gran would say if she knew. I know what we are doing is right, but I know she wouldn't agree."

Rhia reached out and put a hand on Mark's shoulder, "Mark. That speaks volumes about your courage. I know you wouldn't be here if you didn't care. You may not fit the mold of the kind of people most would think are doing this, but that is why you being here is such a big deal. I think what you're doing is pretty brave, and so does my brother and so does Richard. We all value what you do greatly. Don't worry Mark, we've got this."

Mark looked up and considered what Rhia had just told him. 'She's the one who's been in the driver's seat, has done all these amazing things, and she thinks I'm brave? Well, maybe I am,' he thought to himself. Between her and Richard, all the fear that had been plaguing him just an hour before was gone.

Once the whole crew had shown up, they took off to the

raid site with Mark firmly in stride. He left the meeting spot with a sense of courage and importance that he had never felt before. As they made their way, Mark held his gun close. He figured that even if he had to use it, there'd be no way he'd miss anyone–not with him feeling like this. Mark felt like if someone shot him, the bullets would just bounce off of him. They wouldn't make him feel that way if they thought he was a liability. Plus, every previous adventure had gone off without anything happening to him or any of his friends.

The fog bothered him a little, but he was determined to put it out of his mind.

"We've prepared for this situation. It's not a problem. We'll just be a little slower this time, like Gregory said" he said to Richard, more to reassure himself.

"Exactly! Look at you, my *courageous* friend. I was about to say the same thing!" Richard replied, encouragingly.

The raid began like the others. Mark tailed behind, just as he had the previous times. He would jump in the truck once it was secured. He'd make sure that the guards weren't raising their guns as they took off. They were all things he had practiced in his head at least a hundred times.

But, things took a hard turn quickly thereafter. He heard Gregory yell, but couldn't quite make out what.

He could see the trucks outlined through the fog. Whatever Gregory had yelled caused several of the people out in front of him to turn and run back in the direction they had come. As the crowd in front of him thinned and the fog shifted, he could see that there were a large number of soldiers waiting for them with rifles at the ready. All at once the whole scene was flooded with light and a split second later the gunfire started. Many of the people in front of him hadn't fled at Gregory's words. They had their rifles up and firing, the sound was deafening.

For a moment he raised his rifle to add to the fire, but the soldiers' bullets were tearing into his companions in front of him. 'There is brave and there is stupid,' he thought to himself as he turned to look to see if Richard and Rhia had fled. Mark felt a little better about his reservation when he saw that both of them were looking around as well, clearly thinking along the same lines that he was. They all exchanged shocked glances. As more of their friends fell under the barrage of bullets, Rhia tapped Richard on the shoulder and the two of them took off running. Mark took off a split second later to follow them.

'No way. This, this can't be. We had everything planned out! We can't fail to these shitbrains, can we?' Mark thought to himself while running.

Mark heard the cry of a woman's voice ring out over top of the gunfire they had just run from. Richard, just a few feet in front of Mark, was still running and must not have heard her. Mark stopped, turned around, and looked around for the origin of the cry. Between the killing pit they had been standing in and the safety they were running towards, Mark could see the outline of a woman hunched over on her knees. Her cries were louder to him than the gunfire.

All at once it wasn't just some concept of revolution to Mark. One of his fellow rebels needed his help. She was as good as dead even if they captured her alive. Richard was twenty feet in front of him, but Mark screamed "Cover me!"

Mark saw Richard stop and turn to look, but Mark had already made up his mind and charged back to save her. He heard Richard yell something to him, but Mark didn't hear what Richard was trying to say. In the moment, he knew that he had to do what was right-even his Gran couldn't argue that.

Once Mark got back to the woman, she was sitting on her knees. A gun sat next to her. Four guards surrounded her. One of the guards spoke to her in a deep voice, "Play stupid games, win stupid prizes. Hate to say it, but you're not getting out of here. We have orders. We can't let anyone escape. That includes you."

Mark reached her side a split second before the men had raised their rifles. He called out to her, "If you go down, I am going down with you."

Mark lifted his gun and emptied his clip in the direction of the armed men. Many of the shots fired true and three of the guards crumpled. The fourth guard, slightly behind the other three, took aim at Mark who was scrambling to reload.

The man had a snarl on his face, "You little shit. You thought you were going to get away with this? You thought you'd be the hero? Now all you're gonna be is dead." Before Mark could reload, bullets ripped through his chest. Richard saw it happen, almost in slow motion. He aimed at the guard and fired–the guard fell, but it was too late.

Mark fell to the ground and could feel the world closing in on him like a cold vacuum. He was vaguely aware that Richard was lingering over him. In the distance he could hear scattered gunshots through the cold numb ringing in his ears. A vague awareness that he had almost stopped breathing was punctuated by the thought that many of his new friends were meeting the same fate that he was so near to meeting. Even with the understanding that these moments would be his last, Mark's beautiful heart was more concerned with the fate of his friends. He was glad Richard was still alive and that he was at least with his best friend in the end.

Hovering over Mark's seemingly lifeless body, Richard uttered the last words Mark would ever hear; "Mark! I love you. You are my best friend, maybe my only friend! You won't die in vain. You won't die in vain. You didn't die in..." Choking up and struggling to get the words out, Richard trailed off and looked to the sky as if in prayer. Rhia came to his side and told him they needed to get going and fast.

"Richard, come on now. We don't have any more time here. We have to get back!"

"I can't just leave him," Richard begged.

"I understand, love, but we need to move. We won't do him any good by getting ourselves killed. I'm sorry, I really am—but we need to go, NOW!"

Richard touched Mark's face, looked at him one last time and disappeared in the shadows with Rhia. Mark wished he could have told Richard it was ok and to carry on, but his body was paralyzed by death's embrace. All that was left for Mark was the final bow in all its certainty. At least Mark had heard Richard's words.

Mark could hear boots approaching as his lungs struggled to delay the inevitable. Knowing these breaths would be his last, his mind turned to the totality of his short life. Even though he had only known them for a short time, he was grateful for the friends he had made. Most of his life he had been friendless in a cruel world. Mark had also lived his life fearful of just about everything and everyone in it. It was of some comfort that he had finally found courage and that his life, however short, had come to mean something. The most comforting thought of all was that he knew that what he had done was right.

The swirling fog of the night was amplified by his eyes beginning to cloud. The cold gave way to an all-encompassing warmth. In that moment he could see his Gran reaching out through the veil into this world that had all but faded. Far from scorn for his recklessness, she had a look of deep and sincere pride. Mark had become a hero. A boot stood on his chest, a gun was pointed at his head, and a bullet was fired.

Chapter 30

After the survivors had fled a comfortable distance from the massacre, Gregory called them to a stop. Richard looked around at the faces of the remaining would-be rebels of their band of once-merry men and women. A few (himself included) looked lost and were clearly still in shock; most (Rhia included) were clearly solemn, but also wore a look of anger and concentration; Gregory, Old Dirge, and a few of the others had a look of fiery defiance like nothing in the world would or could stop them from getting justice and/or revenge for what had just happened–all had been hardened in a single moment in a barrage of bullet fire.

Richard's mind was everywhere all at once. Everything he had ever said to Mark, everything they had ever done, and everywhere they had ever been cascaded in his mind. The memories of his friend were overpowering the events of the last hour so much so that he had not even begun to think of what would come next. Rhia comforted him by rubbing her hand gently across his back while they all waited for someone to break the silence.

Naturally, Gregory was the first one to speak; "If anyone wants out, I completely understand. I won't think less of anyone that wants to run as far away as they can and never look back. I asked you to be part of a targeted resistance, not to become soldiers in a war and this is no longer a matter of resistance. " Many of the group looked at the ground and contemplated their own defeat and survival.

Gregory continued, "This is not the place to talk of the next steps. Anyone who wants to leave, my blessings go with you-for the rest, let's get to the Rud and plan how we make our stand." He straightened up and gave a formal military salute before turning without any further ceremony and marched in the direction of The Rud.

Old Dirge and Gregory's military looking friends followed him without hesitation. He and Rhia lingered for a moment as the rest of the group wrestled with what to do. A few silently took steps backward and left in different directions. Rhia stood in front of Richard, put her arms around his neck, and stared up at him with her eyes absolutely glowing. He hadn't entirely processed what

Gregory had said until he found himself staring back at those beautiful stars. Even the tragedy that had befallen them had done little to dim the spark in her that he so dearly loved.

Grim resolve overtook him. Mark was gone and, like his mother and father, was never coming back; but Rhia stood in front of him very much alive as was Gregory and Old Dirge.

"I suppose we should catch up to them," Richard said, voice wavering. She didn't say a word, just hugged him and turned to follow in the direction of her brother. Richard turned to look at the rest of the group. One by one they followed her. He followed the second group at the rear, mind still struggling to make sense of what had happened and what was to come.

It was very late when they caught up to Gregory at the Rud. The bar was nearly empty–the last few night owls (most of whom Richard had drank late into the night with on many occasions), the owner of the bar pouring drinks, and their little band of defeated rebels. The way the owner looked at them with genuine sympathy when they came in (Old Dirge must have told him what happened) brought a wave of emotion for his recently departed friend. Gregory stood silently drinking a beer, the wheels in his mind clearly turning fast. Old Dirge, whose animated ramblings had lit up the bar for so many years, sat closely beside where Gregory stood. He was completely sober and his eyes had a look of clear purpose that Richard had never seen in him before. Some of the group ordered a drink before congregating around Gregory.

When everyone had assembled, Gregory snapped back to his immediate surroundings and surveyed the remaining people before starting in; "I cannot properly express my sorrow for the events of this evening, nor properly commemorate those who fell." He looked directly at Richard and gave a somber nod before continuing, "But if we allow despair to set in, they will have fallen for nothing. War was not the goal, but war was always a possibility. Would that we could have inspired enough to rise up before the loss of life, solidarity may have won the day without the unnecessary shedding of blood. As is, what ifs don't matter.

I would be remiss if I didn't admit that I had planned for such a turn of events. Those of you that have taken part of our resistance up to this point have largely been average citizens and I confess this was by design. It was important to show that common everyday people could stand up for a just cause and disrupt the powers to be. I have kept a larger, more military minded, group out of the action to this point so as not to draw us unnecessarily forward into the open and armed conflict of a true rebellion. We number in the hundreds, with many more beginning to train everyday. With this confrontation upon us, the number will quickly grow to the thousands.

This larger force stands armed and ready as we speak, to make a stand in the streets and draw the military into a conflict they will be hard-pressed to win. Such is the way of rebellion, every man or woman that falls in the name of our cause becomes a martyr to inspire a dozen more to join in their wake. I have already sent word to my father begging him to aid the rebellion by, at the very least, convincing as many men as he can to stand down and not join in the killing of citizens. Our true fight is not with the rank and file soldiers, they are every bit as suffocated by the powers to be as anyone else."

Rhia had bristled at the mention of their father, she had been intentionally avoiding thinking of what his part in what to come would be. Richard grabbed her hand and squeezed it, though it did little to alleviate the thought.

Gregory's tone became more matter of fact as he laid out the details of what he envisioned came next, "Tomorrow at first light, this city will become a warzone. Citizens, rebels, and soldiers alike will pay the ultimate price for change. This war won't be quick and it will be anything but painless. I grew up on my father's stories and he never minced words that war is a special kind of hell. The resolve that I ask from any and all that will join me is not to be taken lightly. A great many of us will die, though it will not be in vain. We march for a world where so many thousands don't needlessly suffer and die under the weight of a system that could easily take care of them. A world where justice returns and dignity for the average person can again be realized.

The weight of his words hung on the group as he finished by saying, "I will give everyone one more chance to get out of this and run as far away from this as possible. Nobody will think anything less of anyone who turns from the horrors to come." Unlike the first time he offered the same, nobody moved and nobody wavered.

Old Dirge was the first to speak, "I can't speak for the rest of you, but I've had enough of this world as it is. I'd gladly trade my kingdom for a chance at a better future. I've had a long enough life so I'm ready for whatever comes next." He grabbed the nearest drink to him and raised it to toast, "To death and the promise of a better world."

Richard found himself joining the group in the macabre toast to the cause that they would lend their fragile lives to. Everyone in the room, even the few people who had been in there before the remnants of the group showed up, joined together in somber solidarity. Drinks flowed as everyone made the best of what may be any of their last nights alive. Old Dirge paraded around his kingdom in a kind of silly requiem fitting for a man who had lived a life as strange as his had been.

In the midst of the commiseration, Richard found himself sitting at a table with Gregory and Rhia. They exchanged tense words about their father as it had taken Rhia completely aback that Gregory would think to ask him to get involved.

"You have spent years criticizing him, do you seriously think he would jeopardize everything he has ever worked for his whole life to join a cause he almost certainly would believe is doomed to fail?" She shot at Gregory incredulously.

"Obviously he might just wave it off and do his duty, but we aren't out anything by asking for his help. The worst thing he can do is say no and we are still faced with the same uphill battle." He said, trying to reassure her.

"We?" She exclaimed, "From where I'm sitting it looks like you got us into this predicament and, by the sound of it, less than unintentionally! Lambs to the slaughter for the cause..." she stared daggers at him for a moment, before the weight of the situation bent her anger into concern.

Taking the small win, Gregory pressed; "It wasn't intentionally, but it was always a possibility and the cause *is* just. My sins in orchestrating this are mine and mine alone and I will pay penance whenever it comes due, but something had to force this world to a point of reckoning. Nothing changes if nothing changes."

Richard spoke up, not as an accusation but reflecting on the sad fact of the matter, "Mark's life was quite the price to pay." Both Gregory and Rhia dropped their hostility and looked at Richard with genuine sadness.

"Richard, I can't even begin to say how sorry I am...he was

too good for this world." Gregory's voice wavered, the first time Richard had ever heard him fight back tears.

"He knew you loved him very much and most go their whole lives without ever making a friendship like you two had." Rhia's eyes filled with silent tears and she wrapped her arms around Richard.

Richard began to cry. The type of tears he had shed for his father when Richard was younger, the kind of tears he was already too callous to shed for his mother, the kind of tears where a void in your life that you know will never be filled again leaves you choking for air. Gregory wrapped an arm around the two of them and they all sat embracing while Richard let his emotions run their course.

When he had cried himself out, he grabbed his drink and raised it to his friend; "Mark was the best of us and he went out a hero, which is more than any of the shitbrains will ever be able to say." The other two raised their glasses as well.

After a few moments of silence to honor Mark–Gregory stood up and patted Richard on the back before giving Rhia a hug, then turned to address the rest of the rebels gathered in the bar.

"It's very late and the fighting will begin early tomorrow; everyone should get some sleep. For those of you who want to join me in this fight, meet me at first light where I gave my speech those few short moons ago. For those of you that want to sit this one out,

I salute you and it has been an honor."

Everyone made to finish their drinks and bid goodbye to their companions (some for the evening, some forever). Richard and Rhia went to do the same. Gregory doubled back and asked Richard, "Can I talk to you alone for just a moment?"

Richard followed him a few feet away and Gregory spoke in a hushed but earnest tone, "I need to ask a huge favor from you." He took Richard's silence for agreement, "Will you take my sister and leave the city?" Richard was startled and made to protest, but Gergory continued; "I know both of you would fight and fight bravely, but this is more a matter of strategy than sentimentality- though I confess both do factor into why I'm asking this of you.

You are smart enough to tell others what you have seen. In the fight ahead many will die and we will need many more to rally to the cause and take their places. Rhia is my father's daughter, the fearless and beautiful daughter of a decorated General combined with your ability to remember what you have witnessed here can do more for the cause by spreading the message of hope than you could ever hope to do by acting as fodder for bullets.

I cannot tell you enough how sorry I am that Mark cannot accompany you and I will bear the weight of his death until I meet my own, whether that is tomorrow or many years from now. Personal attachments do not make for a good commander and the weight of worrying about the two of you would guarantee I would not be at my best when it comes to making decisions. I do not want you nor my sister dying in the streets at the hand of some rank and file soldier. Please Richard, I ask you as a friend and brother."

Richard let the request sink in and contemplated for a moment before replying, "I can do my best, but she obviously has a will of her own. It's why I love her as much as I do. '

"I know that, but she *also* knows that. She loves us both and I'm certain that she will see the truth behind the request."

"Why don't you just ask her?" Richard asked honestly.

"Because it's best if it comes from you, Richard. I'm not asking you to just run away, I'm asking you to take care of each other and keep the flame of this rebellion and the hope for change alive. You both will be far beyond my reach to protect, so she has to do it because she believes that the two of you can be there for each other long enough to succeed. I may not be here in 24 hours; you are all that either of you have left now." He reached his massive hand out for Richard to shake. Richard reached out his own and took a long look at the bravest person he had ever met for what could be the last time.

Before waiting for Richard to say anything Gregory walked over to Rhia, wrapped his arms around her, picked her up and spun her around. He kissed her on the forehead and said a brief and casual goodbye before leaving the Rud.

Richard returned to Rhia's side. She asked him, "What did he want to tell you?" Richard put his arms around her waist and pulled her close as he watched Gregory fade into the night.

"It can wait just a bit. I'll tell you when we make it back to my dorm." He said, taking in everything he could about the moment.

"I suppose your dorm is the best place to go right now all things considered, *thanks for asking*," she replied with a little bit of lighthearted sarcasm.

The two of them said goodbye to Old Dirge who gave Richard a look as if to say 'it has been nice knowing you' before making their way out of The Rud, into the night, and back towards his dorm.

Chapter 31

The Old General sat at his desk in the ornate office of his manor in the early hours of the morning. Normally he would be fast asleep, but reports had been coming in all night that a group of soldiers accompanying a food and rations caravan had come under heavy fire by a band of armed rebels. Final casualty numbers were yet to be determined, but the estimate was at least a dozen soldiers and several dozen rebels. The men and the operation were not under his command so there was no sense of urgency to know the exact details. His attention was on the evolving orders coming from the top brass above him, as well as inquiries from his top officers about what they should be preparing for.

For his entire career he had sympathized with the plight of

the common person and had made his reputation as one of the token people in power who advocated on their behalf. He had always known that armed rebellion was inevitable, but as the years had passed, he had come to hope that he would pass of old age or illness before the day came that he would be forced by duty to abandon his sympathies and take part in orchestrating the brutal response necessary to quell such a rebellion. The totality of it all hung on him. As the survivor of many bloodied campaigns in his youth, he knew exactly what fate awaited on the streets of the city come morning.

With each passing minute, the time dwindled down to where he would have to walk downstairs and give orders to the top officers under his command. The orders from the top were not set in stone as of yet. Details of the firefight were clearly still being discovered and, while all of the communications he had received so far had all urged some measure of military engagement, the extent of the brutality that would be suggested was being debated by people with more political concerns than he had.

Through the years he had been meticulous about only lending his prestige to men (for sake of promotion) that he believed were of as good a conscience as a career military person could have, as well as being men who would see wisdom in his mentorship. He saw many of them as sons. Much like his own son, many of them were quick to question the ethical integrity of various parts of the system–unlike his son, they were not hotheaded and predisposed to insubordination. He knew that there would be some protests if he were to ultimately forward the order to join in fighting against their own citizens, but he knew that they would ultimately do their duty should he ask it of them.

With all of the worries of command weighing heavy, he was further weighed down by concern for his children. He had always kept a close eye on both of them, but after Gregory was expelled from the middle management college he had been hard pressed to find information about his activities without raising suspicion about what he believed his son to be doing. Rhia had also become elusive as of late.

The General had done his best to allow his daughter space to explore and grow into her own. He loved both of his children, but Gregory was too much like himself for his own comfort–Rhia on the other hand was his pride and joy. Rhia's evening adventures had not troubled him greatly at first because he knew more than anyone else just how resourceful and clever she really was. She had always been a prodigy at anything put in front of her. Tutors over the years had all written glowing summaries of their lessons. It didn't matter if it was mathematics, martial arts, or music–she had a natural talent at things that made him more proud than anything else in his life ever had. She was absent now and his stomach turned with worry that she may end up caught up in the fighting on the streets if she did not return shortly.

His worrisome reflections were cut short by a knock at his door. He was fairly surprised as he had not been expecting to be bothered by anything other than the phone call when the final orders came down from the top brass. After taking a brief moment to shuffle some of the more sensitive papers on his desk back into covered folders, he called out; "Enter."

One of his promising Captains opened the door and held it open while standing at attention to allow a man in civilian clothing (a modest but not cheap suit and tie) to enter the room. In the dim light in the middle of the night, the General immediately recognized the man to be the Dean of the college his son had attended until recently.

"This gentleman says he is a close friend and requests an audience with you, sir," the Captain called out formally.

"This gentleman speaks the truth. Thank you Captain. You are dismissed," The General replied with a mixture of familiarity to The Dean and formality to his officer. The Captain quickly and efficiently left and closed the door behind him.

The General motioned for the man to take a seat before asking, "To what do I owe this visit in the middle of the night, Dean? I hadn't expected to hear from you anytime soon considering my son no longer attends your school."

The Dean was intentionally keeping a professional and businesslike demeanor, but it was undercut by the severity of the situation he was about to bring to the attention of his old friend, The General. He took more time than the situation warranted to deliberately arrange himself in the chair.

Not out of a childlike impatience nor to be dismissive from his position of power, but out of sincere worry as to why The Dean would go to all the trouble to visit him in the middle of the night-the General pressed, "I trust you are not here with good news." The Dean's eyes fell, so The General added; "It's alright, very few people bring good news anymore," to ease the tension of the situation by playing to the familiarity between the two.

The Dean looked up with resolve, "You are correct that I do not come with good news." The General nodded, ready to hear whatever the situation was. The Dean began in earnest, "The news is in regard to your son and, as much as it pains me to inform you, your daughter as well." While the mention of his daughter made his stomach turn over, The General maintained a look of problem-solving concentration.

"As you know from the last time that we spoke when your son offered himself up to be expelled, my ability to monitor him directly was greatly diminished. However, he maintained contact with several of my other students. With one of which, your daughter has apparently begun a relationship of sorts." The Dean allowed the information to sink in, trying to read his old friend.

The General was practiced at not showing his personal thoughts and asked, as if for strategic clarity, "I trust there was a good reason that you had not informed me of this sooner?"

The Dean was not alarmed nor defensive and spoke to his friend like an equal, "Several good reasons actually. First and foremost, I had my suspicions before that the girl my student had been bringing back to my dormitories was in fact your daughter, based on the general description–but didn't want to draw attention to our affiliation by making a hard inquiry into it. Secondly, there was no pressing reason (outside of drawing the disapproval out of an overly protective and well connected father) to inform you. Idle gossip about my friends' children's romantic habits is a practice I avoid if at all possible."

The General ignored the banter about idle gossip and stuck straight to the details, "There wasn't a pressing reason, but there is one now."

"There certainly is. I was informed a few hours ago that one of my students, a student that your son has maintained contact with, was amongst the casualties in the firefight earlier this evening. The student found dead was also a close confidant of the other student with whom your daughter has been visiting in the late hours of the night. Shortly before I came to personally tell you of your children's involvement, she was seen returning to my campus with him."

The Dean's whole persona wore the air of deep concern befitting a professional man telling an old friend bad personal news, but he focused his eyes intently on the General—hoping that his old friend would spare him the telling of as many details as possible by filling in as much as he could. He was content to allow the General as much time to process the implications of the news as his old friend wanted.

The General maintained his learned and practiced stoicism, but his mind connected the dots as to how bad the situation really was for himself, The Dean, his children, and all parties involved. Treasonous rebellion would be met with summary executions; not only for the rebels, but for anyone and everyone who had played a part in allowing it to fester. In the decades leading up to this point, the government had taken progressively more brutally authoritarian measures to quell any attempts to undermine their power.

In the early years, as he was climbing the ranks, the fall of the common man was the result of casual indifference to their suffering by the people with the power to change policy and allocate resources. His own rise in status was because his military career had taught him how to express sympathy for a concern while simultaneously falling back on following orders to maintain some semblance of status quo. He was often quoted by news outlets for the sympathetic things he would say, inevitably accompanied by a photograph of him with political leaders when they were signing something into law that was in direct conflict with his expressed values–very intentionally to show that even a sympathetic man like him saw sense in measures that favored only a privileged few.

As the years went by, the policies of the rich and powerful became more brazen and (eventually) the need to parade a man like him in front of the public eye to soften the blow was no longer needed because there was no reasonable chance that common people could do anything about it, even if they had tried. He had met the Dean many years ago at a conference for young(ish) professionals that operated in the city in a very public attempt to make it look like the powers-that- be were going to try to "fix things." It was a time before the ruling elite had given up on pretending that they had a plan to stop the systemic institutional decline. The two had bonded over the cynical observation that it was an elaborate show with no real directive.

In the first few years of their friendship, it had become amply clear that the government was not going to lift a finger to make life better for common people. The Dean had introduced him to a network of politicians, business leaders, civil servants, and community organizers that sought to push the issue of reform from the fringes of power that they did hold. He had met dozens of their little coalition over the years, always making sure to stay a politically safe distance from any members that sought to push the issue of change with too much zeal. His primary duties were to the Armed Services and his family. The political movement was a matter for others more suited to the task, his best contribution to the cause was to use his reputation to try and make sure that the military did not become a mindless tool for the elite to use at whim.

His instincts to maintain distance from the political arm of their movement paid off (personally) when a large number of their group had pressed the legislature on the need for drastic and immediate reforms. The calls for protest combined with a forward lobbying attempt where the would-be reformers did not mince words about the need for change, even when met with indifference by legislators, was seen as a step too far. Leaders that had dared to align themselves with the movement were branded as traitors and rebels and were arrested or disappeared in an attempt to dissuade anyone from hoping to challenge the status quo again. He had privately condemned the actions as unethical overreach, but publicly maintained his commitment to maintain the status quo and protect the order within the ranks of the military.

The temperance of his approach had won very small victories. When the military was used to put down a hunger protest, he made enough of a complaint that the government looked for different ways to deter future protests. It was in the wake of not wanting the military involved in brutal crackdowns that the idea for the Citizens Watch was first proposed. In its initial conception, the legislature had wanted to use it to kill two birds with one stone by releasing non-political violent offenders from their overburdened prison system to fill the roles. The General had found enough sympathetic allies to eventually change the proposal to fill the Citizen Watch with people who were rejected from police or military service.

Many times over the years, he had quietly wrestled with self-doubt as to whether his approach was the right one or if he was so caught up with surviving that he had abandoned his principles. It didn't matter now. His children had forced him to a moment of decision that he had spent his whole life trying to avoid. The government had dropped any pretense of justice and anybody they deemed affiliated with the rebels involved in tonight's firefight would meet a traitors' end.

As he looked back at his friend, The Dean, he considered the practical details of the situation before breaking the silence; "I don't see any way that my children's involvement doesn't lead to our public execution when the investigation into this rebellion is concluded." The Dean maintained his aura of solemn professionalism and his lack of reaction to The General's words was due to the fact that he had already reached the same conclusion.

In a display of gallows humor and to break the suffocating tension of their current reality, The General asked a joking question; "I don't suppose I'd be lucky enough that the student who died was the one who pulled my Rhia into this mess?"

Both men forced a chuckle before The Dean replied, "I can't even give you that." He allowed the joke its moment before continuing, "You may not be as disappointed in the young man as you think. He is the son of one of our former coalition members and, while being quite the example of youthful angst, is generally a bright individual. In a different world, or even a different time, you might actually have liked him. I don't know him personally, but everything I've seen in keeping tabs on him suggests that he is his father's son."

"Did I know his father?" The General asked with genuine curiosity.

"I doubt that the two of you were ever in the same room as he was quite the critical writer as well as the mover-shaker type of political organizer. He was, in no small way, responsible for that last attempt to force reforms that resulted in so many being arrested. Your boundaries on your involvement in our movement being as they were, it was never an acquaintance I sought to make for you. Nevertheless, you would have liked his father if you had ever met him. He was as brilliant and charismatic as he was hopelessly optimistic. I dare say, he might have even swayed your modest temperament."

"Rhia is a very capable young woman, I would fully expect

her to know what she was doing. I did my part to raise her and being able to trust her ability to care for herself is the best I can salvage given the circumstances..." The General trailed off as cracks in his stoicism were being filled with the emotion of a father placed in an unthinkable position.

The Dean sat in quiet sympathy while The General processed. After a few moments of reflection–The General rolled his eyes, forced a grim smile, and said; "quite the mess we find ourselves in."

"A mess indeed," The Dean agreed.

"The mess has been made, the battle is upon us, all that is left to do is to decide our parts in it. Have you decided what you are going to do? Of the two of us, you have the better chance of running away and disappearing into obscurity. You could be half the world away before your involvement is ever found out." The General was ever a practical man.

"It is an option, but not a satisfactory one. Though, my plan largely depends on what you decide to do."

The General's curiosity was piqued by the suggestion that their fates were intertwined. "How do you mean?" he asked.

"It is only a matter of time before my now deceased student leads to an inquiry into the school's involvement and, as a result, my personal involvement in allowing your son and your daughter's love interest special favors in remaining enrolled at the school despite their many actions that would lead any other student to expulsion. Your son is not the only child of a powerful bureaucrat to make problems at my school, but he received more leeway than is afforded by status alone.

In my heart, I feel that running is a young man's game. I can't honestly tell myself I would be living to fight another day because if I don't make a stand here and now, then I never will. My school has enough non-perishable food, fuel, and other provisions that it could serve as a safehouse in the coming war on the streets for quite some time. Strategically, it has many sturdy buildings that could be repurposed for emergency housing. An oasis from the fighting in the streets for soldiers and rebels alike. If it was reinforced by the men under your command, it would be difficult for the government to overtake without carpet bombing their own city and looking foolish by killing their own soldiers.

It would allow for you to appear to take a temperate stance by dedicating your force to mitigating the suffering and loss of human life within the city, while allowing you to subtly back your son and the rebellion he has found himself embroiled in. A public declaration of practical application of martial law on your part, until the fighting has ended, would endear you to the heart of every sympathizer against the brutality of our government as of late. It would at least allow us the hope that the rebellion wins out and that we never face the hung tribunal that certainly awaits should we do nothing."

The General sat in silence as he contemplated The Dean's proposal. A spark of hope lay at the center of the plan, but The General was not ignorant at the loss of life that would accompany the plan's success. If he ordered his men to operate as a rogue force solely out of his own desire to spare himself and his children then his moral compass would not even allow himself to consider it, but the proposition had broader implications. He had known for a very long time that the system that he served had absolutely no plans to ever change to right the wrongs of so many years of greed and decadence. This was a matter of life and death for more than just himself and the people he cared about most, it was a matter of life and death for everyone who hadn't had a chance in years.

"Very well thought out," The General mused.

"Necessity is the mother of all innovation, they say. That doesn't sound like a no." The Dean replied, daring to hope for the first time since hearing the news that a student of his was among the rebels killed earlier in what now felt like an endless night.

"I see no other way." The General said as a matter of fact. "I will formalize my orders, gather my men, and issue my public statement before morning. Expect men to begin arriving before first light."

The Dean stood up and made to shake The General's hand, "Thank you."

"Don't thank me yet," said The General as he got up and shook The Dean's hand. "There is much to do in a few short hours, but before you go I have a favor to ask of you."

The Dean looked back at his friend with a look of extreme gratitude and answered with a single word, "Anything."

"If my daughter is still there when you return, I ask that you go and speak to her and the boy with her. It is bad enough that my son will likely give his life, though the cause is arguably just. I cannot bear the thought that I should lose them both." He got up, walked over to a safe that was inconspicuously blocked from the line of sight when entering the door by a file cabinet, and fiddled with the combination to open it. The General pulled out a small stack of official looking documents and thumbed through them until he found what he was looking for. He put the rest back and grabbed a small stack of cash before closing the safe and walking back over to The Dean.

"These are government and military identifications that should allow her to get a safe distance away before any questions are asked," he handed the cash and identifications to The Dean, "Please persuade her to leave before first light. Have her take the boy with her if she must, but it is important that she lives to fight another day. Even if we must make *our* stand, there has to be some hope this isn't the *last* stand should we fail. Please tell her I love her and I am proud of her."

With a final shake of their hands, The Dean turned and left. He was gone for less than 60 seconds when there was another knock on his door. Believing it to be The Dean returning to say some forgotten thing, he opened the door himself. Much to his surprise, he found himself face to face with the promising young captain.

"Sir!" The Captain snapped to attention.

"At ease." The General ordered.

"You have another visitor, Sir. He is unarmed and was stopped at your gates. He claims he has news he can only relay to you."

"Bring him here."

"Sir." The Captain saluted before walking down the hallway to relay the order. The General left his door open and returned to his chair. He allowed himself to contemplate the enormity of the task in front of him, his men, the city, and their world as a whole. While waiting for his second surprise guest, he began to write out formal orders. After a few short minutes the Captain returned with a young man escorted by two of his soldiers.

As the ensemble entered the room, the Captain stood in salute and the armed soldiers stood at attention. The General looked the young man in their custody up and down, recognizing that he resembled the type of boys his son regularly befriended. Sensing no harm or plot to deceive him, The General spoke to his men; "You may wait outside the door with your men, Captain."

"Sir," replied the Captain who dropped his salute, waited for his men to step outside, and left, closing the door behind him.

Once the other soldiers had left the room, the young man saluted The General and then stood at attention while saying; "Sir, I have news from your son." The General had suspected as much and began writing on a piece of paper.

The young man stood there patiently waiting for The General to reply. Once the General had finished what he was writing, he looked up at the young man and asked; "What news do you bring, son?"

"Permission to hand The General a letter, sir."

"Granted."

The young man dug a letter out of his pocket, stepped forward, and handed it to The General. It was a single piece of paper folded in half. The General opened it, read it, and re-read it. It confirmed what he suspected all along–that his son had not merely been caught up in the rebellion, but rather had been the one who orchestrated it. All that it contained was a brief description of Gregory's part in coordinating the attack and a plea to his father to "come to his senses and do what is right."

The General made a mental note to remind himself to tell Gregory (should he see him again) that the note had no bearing on his decision to come to his aid so as not to further inflate Gregory's ego. He had already written his reply to his son before reading the request. Without any further explanation; he folded his own letter requesting that Gregory (and whomever followed him) to meet up with his forces near the school, or at least send a messenger before first light in the morning–and handed it to the young man.

"Take this to my son," The General Ordered.

The young man saluted The General and said, "Yes, General." The General rolled his eyes and halfheartedly saluted him back before calling for the Captain to have the young man escorted safely back off of the premises.

When the door finally closed, he slumped into his chair and returned to writing out his formal plans. The General suspected that most of the officers directly under his command would follow his orders without question, both because they were men of conscience and because of their personal respect for his command. He was confident that the few who may harbor reservations could be easily reasoned with because he had done his due diligence when deciding who to promote under his command and ultimately was asking them to, as his son put it, "do the right thing."

He hoped against hope that his declaration of martial law, rather than obey the inevitable orders from above to wage an unrelenting war against their own citizens with whatever means necessary, would resonate with other Generals and high ranking commanders. The military, at its core, has a sacred duty to protect the civil structure of society and he was fully prepared to go to any lengths to fulfill that duty. There were no grand delusions in his mind that all other commanders would see the moral imperative to protect citizens rather than to obey the mad orders of a failing ruling class. He was the token sympathizer, rather than the rule. Still, if he could hold out long enough to be joined by even a few others–it very well might unravel the last bit of control that the failed system could wield.

It was to be a very long night in a series of very long nights to come. The General prepared for war.

Chapter 32

Richard sat in the chair at his desk. He was nursing a glass of whiskey and staring blankly at the wall next to his bed as the images of the horrors of the night replayed in front of him as if displayed onto a screen from a projector. Rhia sat on the bed with her arms wrapped around her knees, half-looking at the covers of Richard's books which he had arranged on a bookshelf. Keeping her mind occupied was all that she could do to stop from succumbing to the sorrow welling up inside of her.

She had held it together well enough as friends and companions had fallen around her and had even stayed pragmatic when talking to her brother and the other survivors in The Rud, but as the hours had dragged on deep into the night the veneer of composure became more and more difficult to maintain. The foolishness of their plan was evident in hindsight and she still harbored a pained resentment to think that Mark and all of the others who had died, did so in service of her brother's ambition. Everyone involved knew the risks and she still knew that the cause was just, but righteousness wouldn't bring Mark back.

Richard was the worse for the wear of the two. He was still in complete shock and he had visibly shut down entirely. Tears weren't enough to alleviate the pain of the loss he felt. Underneath the pain, he also felt extremely guilty. If Mark hadn't met him, if he hadn't ever come to this wretched school, if he had just minded his business and endured the misery of the world on his own-then Mark would be alive and well on his way to becoming a lower middle manager. For so many years he had been utterly certain that the degenerate world needed to change at all costs, but now that he knew what the real cost was, he would give anything for things to have been different.

Rhia looked over and saw the torture that was going on inside Richard's head as well as the paralysis from the crushing weight of the tragic and sudden turn of events. On many occasions, she had heard her father describe battlefield paralysis and the effects of shellshock. He was not in immediate danger, but he was showing all the signs of both. It was enough to make her get up and tend to him. She crossed over to the desk to pour herself a drink, before topping off his mostly untouched glass.

He was clearly somewhere else as he didn't register that she had gotten up and filled his glass until she grabbed his hand and gave it a little squeeze. Richard looked at her in a daze, so she pulled on his arm and said, "Come sit with me on the bed. I know it might feel too soon, but it would probably help us to talk. If not about what happened, just getting out of your head for a moment would be good for you." Richard was in no shape to argue, so he got up and sat with her on the bed.

The act of getting up and moving returned him to his present surroundings. He took a long drink and his eyes lit up as he remembered that they had a huge decision in front of them and very little time to make it. He cleared his throat and turned to her, "There will be time enough to mourn, but I need to ask you about something Gregory asked of me."

"About whatever he said to you that he didn't want to say to me," she replied, clearly not having forgotten about the last few minutes at The Rud earlier.

"Yes," said Richard, glad that she was thinking more clearly than he was. "He asked us to leave the city together before the fighting starts." She was as taken aback as he had been when Gregory had asked him. He continued, "I immediately thought 'no way in hell,' but he used his Gregory ways to make me really think about the idea. He admitted that some of it was personal and that he didn't want to be worried about us constantly while also fighting a war, but he also said it was strategic."

Rhia rolled her eyes, "*Of course he would say that,* he has always thought of me as his little sister and would say anything to keep me out of danger."

Richard pleaded Gregory's case, "I'm sure that is probably true, but he did make the strategic case sound convincing. You are the daughter of a powerful man and could gather support in other cities."

"Making you, what? My bodyguard? My fuck toy? My babysitter?" She shot back at him.

Richard smiled at the thought and tried a joke to cut into the seriousness of the impossible place that they found themselves in, "That doesn't sound so bad to me." She lightened up a little bit, but gave him a deliberate look as if to say, 'don't push it.' Taking the small victory, Richard relayed the logical reason Gregory had given him to accompany her; "Gregory said that I will remember what I've seen so far and would be helpful in organizing new resistances wherever we would go. Someone to keep the story alive."

The indignation melted away from her as she genuinely considered what her brother was proposing. She had seen Richard grow exponentially in the time that they had been together and he was the type of bright individual that could make a good attempt to recreate what her brother had done. It was not far-fetched to think that the two of them could find willing people anywhere they went who wanted to see change as badly as they did. Her heart plummeted as she realized that Gregory was asking this of them because he was fairly certain he would not live to spread the message himself. The sorrow she had been holding back welled up in her and she began to cry.

Richard took the glass out of her hand and sat both on the desk before returning to the bed, wrapping his arms around her, and holding her while crying with her. The enormity of what lay before them melted away in a flood of tears and, for just a moment, the world shrunk to the size of two young hearts in love-tangled up in the sorrow and remorse of having lived in such an awful time. They sat there for a long while before Rhia pulled away and got up to say that she had to use the restroom.

Richard returned to his desk and began sipping from the glasses in front of him while working out the details of their would-be escape from the city. He didn't even bother to look at his father's watch, he knew the hour was very late and they had an incredibly short amount of time to decide their fate. He was startled back to reality by a knock at his door.

Immediately he thought that it must be Janice. She had been absent from his mind for a while and if she had still been coming to his room to try and bed him, he must have been out with Mark, Gregory, and Rhia or busy with some aspect of the robberies he had been taking part in. With everything that had happened that evening, he was ready to explode, and she would be the perfect outlet for his anger. After all, it was people like her that had allowed the world to get bad enough to where Mark had to die trying to change it. He thundered up from his desk and flew to the door prepared for the confrontation.

Richard threw open the door ready to scream, but stopped in complete disbelief as the visitor was clearly not her. The visitor was a middle-aged man in a modest looking suit holding a briefcase. Richard stood in stunned silence and stared at the man. While the man was not somebody he knew, the man certainly looked familiar to him. The visitor was not surprised to find Richard in a state of confusion and waited patiently for Richard to say something.

After it became clear that Richard was content to stand there staring, the visitor asked in a tone that attempted friendliness despite its overly professional nature; "Would you mind if I came in to talk?" Richard stepped back in silence and gestured for the man to enter the room. Richard closed the door behind the man and went to grab a chair from the corner.

While crossing the room he noticed that he had left his father's revolver laying out on top of his desk. The man did not appear to be any type of law enforcement, but Richard was nervous, nonetheless. He moved the chair across the room, eyeing the man with suspicion; both because a firearm used to kill a soldier lay on his desk as well as the uneasy feeling that he knew the man from somewhere. Nothing in the man's movements or demeanor gave away the purpose for the visit, but the man did not seem to be overly interested in the firearm-not to mention the alcohol next to it, the ashtray full of cigarettes next to his window, nor the books which he had tidied away since Rhia had been coming around.

When Richard had moved the chair a conversational distance from his, the man walked over to it and sat down casually like this was a familiar and frequent occurrence between them. The man waited patiently for Richard to sit and join him in conversation. There was something so surreal about it all that Richard ignored any etiquette. He fished out a cigarette, lit it (the raspy cough had abated lately because he had stopped chain-smoking after he and Rhia began whatever their relationship was), and poured himself a fresh glass of whiskey before finally settling down in the chair to speak to the man.

The man spoke first, "I suppose introductions are in order, though I do know who you are. First and foremost, I was a friend of your parents-but more relevant to the why and when of my arrival this particular evening, I also happen to be The Dean of this school." Richard was dumbfounded. Never in his life had so few words made his head reel from such an insane amount of information to unpack. He stared at The Dean in utter disbelief until the ash tail on his cigarette dropped into his lap. Even then, rather than reply, he brought the ember back to life with a deep inhale before taking a huge gulp of his drink. No amount of cigarette smoke nor alcohol could clear his head to properly process what he had heard.

After it was clear that Richard was not going to offer any follow-up questions, The Dean continued; "I regret to make this formal introduction under such regrettable circumstances. As a matter of security for our school, I was informed earlier this evening that one of my students was found amongst the bodies of an armed group who fired at uniformed soldiers. This young man, one Markus Spillman, happens to be a close friend of yours." Richard's eyes narrowed, wondering if The Dean was *really* here to tell him of his friend's gruesome death or if he was here to accuse him of the crime he had most certainly committed.

The Dean sensed Richard's accusatory look and spoke dismissively, "Judging by your reaction, his passing is not news to you. Whatever your involvement in the matter is not the reason I have come to you now. I am here to uphold the promise that I made to your mother to do everything within my power to protect you." For the second time since returning to his dorm, Richard stared at the wall next to his bed and a memory played for him as if on a screen.

It was the memory of the day the man had come to tell his mother that his father would never be coming back. The same man who had informed his mother sat before him now. It had been a few years and the man had aged, but there was no mistaking that the two were the same person. Twice in the same night, Richard's whole life turned upside down. Just then Rhia returned from the restroom. She stopped in the doorway and widened her stance as if ready to fight The Dean.

The Dean was not fazed by her arrival in the slightest. With a warm look on his face, he turned to speak to her, "Oh good. I was hoping against hope that you were still here. Please sit, I am eager to speak with you as well. I bring word from your father." Richard saw Rhia's face drop into the mind-blown look he imagined he must also be wearing.

Rhia dropped her stance and quietly shut the door before walking over to stand next to where Richard was sitting. She put her hand on his shoulder in an attempt to ground herself back to the reality of the room. The Dean sat comfortably as if he was a close friend who had seen the two of them many times. Richard could feel her intensity out of the corner of his perception as both of them wrestled with the few short words The Dean had spoken so far.

The Dean chuckled and began to explain himself; "As I was just telling Richard, I made a promise to his mother that I would do everything in my power to keep him safe," the two of them exchanged glances (both taking comfort that the other was equally perplexed by the information), "and shortly before making my way here, I paid your father a visit and made him a similar promise.

You see–there was a time, when I was much younger, that I was part of a coalition that sought reform. There were a great many of us back then, including both of your fathers. Both served the cause in very different ways, but I counted both amongst my close friends. We were either too naive or not naive enough, because nothing we did ended up preventing us from ending up where we find ourselves today. For that you have my sincere apology."

Neither Richard nor Rhia could find the words to respond. This was the first time that either had heard anything about their fathers being part of such a group. While both understood it to be true, the revelation changed both of their memories surrounding vague things their fathers had said throughout the years. For Rhia, all of the times her father had assured her brother that he was not merely sitting by and doing nothing made more sense. For Richard, the nature of his father's parties and the night he had spoken at the bar he and Mark had visited had become more clear. They had tried to make change in their own ways.

The Dean continued, "Richard. Have you really never asked yourself, all these years, why none of your antics here at this school have ever so much as led to a formal reprimand?" He had, but not in a million years had he suspected it was because a family friend was looking out for him. "Rhia. Didn't you find it strange that your brother was sent to a middle management school rather

than some ambitious military school fitting your father's position?"
She had, but she had just assumed it was a stunt orchestrated by
Gregory to further disappoint their father.

"I assure you that we believed we were taking the best course
of action by keeping the lot of you as safe as we could, while we
waited and hoped that the opportunity would present itself to push
for the reforms we set out to achieve all those years ago. Leave it to
the young to force the issue. Not that I condemn what you have
done, mind you. We have become too old and too comfortable
and our aspirations have become the things we tell ourselves to
allow ourselves to sleep at night.

For better or worse, war is coming. Any moment now, the
first shots will ring out in what will surely be a bitter and awful
conflict. Perhaps if we had taken bolder stances sooner, all of this
could have been avoided–but it matters little now. I have come here
to fulfill the promises I made to the best of my abilities before the
coming storm." The Dean stopped to fiddle with the lock on the
briefcase.

He opened it in his lap and pulled out some documents and
a bundle of cash. "Your father wanted you to have these Rhia.
They are your government identifications. He wanted me to tell
you that he loves you and is proud of you *and* to ask you, on his
behalf, to use them to leave town before the fighting begins. Your
father and I will have to make our stand here and now, but he

believes that it is important for you to survive in case we fail. He even grudgingly sees the wisdom should Richard choose to accompany you." She took the documents and money from him. The Dean ceremoniously closed the briefcase.

"As for you Richard," The Dean handed him the entire briefcase, "Your parents had left you a handsome sum of money, some of which has been spent on your time here at the school and at your discretion. Your father was quite the prolific writer in his youth and there is more than enough to make your task easier should you choose to accompany Rhia. This case contains as much money as I could come up with for you on such short notice as well as the banking details should you require more.

It also contains the identification card the school has on file as well as a letter your father wrote to you from prison shortly before his passing, which he instructed me to give you when you ventured out on your own. I visited him until the end, but your mother's passing was too much for him to bear. Of all the friends I have lost in my life, his loss affected me the most. He was never the one to advocate for violence, but he would be incredibly proud that you have forced change in your own way." The Dean trailed off, having concluded with the formalities.

"I strongly urge you both to heed the advice put before you. In a few minutes, we will begin the evacuation of the students from this school. In a few short hours, this city will be a war zone. I have offered this school as a staging ground for your father to aid your brother in whatever way he can. Would that I were a younger man, I would offer to accompany you-but it is my time to give my all to the cause as so many I have known have done before.

My best advice, should you be so inclined to listen, is that you leave the city by train. You can get lost in the bustle of people fleeing the fighting, pay in cash, and face minimal scrutiny as to your identities."

Rhia and Richard were glued in place, so The Dean stood up and crossed to Richard's desk; "They will check you for firearms, so I daresay I will need this more than you will in the coming days. Your father always wrestled with why he kept it, but I think that even he knew that this day would come." He picked the revolver up off the desk before reaching out to shake Rhia and Richard's hands, "It's truly a pity to meet under such circumstances and I am deeply sorry to hear about Mark."

He crossed to the door with Richard's father's revolver in hand, "I would make your decision sooner than later, the fighting will start any minute now. Best of luck and Godspeed." The Dean left and shut the door behind him.

Richard looked up at Rhia searching for something to say, struggling where to begin. The look on her face said it all. She had been indignant when Gregory had suggested she flee to safety, but

Richard could see the words The Dean had relayed from her father had achieved their desired effect. He too had been on the fence when Gregory had asked him, but the perspective he had gained in the few hours since had swayed him. The beautiful girl with stars in her eyes that stood before him mattered more to him than vengeance for Mark or chasing glory and possibly a hero's death like Gregory. That they could also do more good spreading the call to rebellion than by dying in the first days of it was every justification he needed.

He packed up a few small things that might make the initial journey easier into a backpack and a cloth bag which he handed to Rhia. She handed him back most of her stack of money to put in the briefcase with the rest. They stopped to take one last drink in the room which he had loathed not so long ago, a small and hurried cheers to the life they were leaving behind. Without any more ceremony, they made their way out into the early morning and towards the train station.

Chapter 33

The dull sun was beginning to rise in the east. Richard and Rhia had wasted no time in crossing the city by the twilight of dawn. The railway depot where they were heading was only a short distance away when the first gunshots rang out in the early morning air. They exchanged glances, but didn't dare to slow their pace. War had begun in the city.

By the time they had arrived at the entrance to the station, scattered gunfire could be heard every few minutes. Neither were military strategists, but it sounded like small skirmishes compared to what they had survived the evening prior.

The sight waiting for them inside surprised them both. It was immediately clear that a fair number of people must have been warned about the coming conflict, as the depot was already crowded-with more people arriving in droves behind them. There was great variation in the appearance of the people making up the scared mob; some (like themselves) had packed lightly, some were lugging what appeared to be everything they could carry with them, some were lone people that seemed only mildly inconvenienced to be leaving a city for which they had no attachment, some were families that had the forlorn look of those abandoning everything they had ever cared about-all were visibly nervous every time bullets fired in the distance.

In the chaos of the swarm of newly made refugees, they could see a long queue had formed leading to the windows where tickets were purchased. Rhia and Richard wasted no time getting themselves to the back of the line. They exchanged nervous glances. Most of the people around them were completely innocent and just fleeing what was quickly becoming a warzone; whereas the two of them were, at least, partially to blame for the misfortune that the strangers around them were now victims of. Both knew that it was highly unlikely that they were already wanted in connection with the robberies, but the tension of the scene added to the nerves that they already felt.

Rhia surveyed the people packing themselves into the already crowded station with genuine sympathy. She voiced concern to Richard, "These are only a fraction of the people who will be caught up in this. The ones who left in time to make it to safety. It breaks my heart to think of the countless others who won't make it out."

Richard was also caught up in the overwhelming weight of so many people fleeing everything they knew. He felt the magnitude of the tragedy played out on the faces of the people around him, but suppressed the urge to get overly sentimental because he knew that there was no going back now; "I hope it will have been worth it," is all he could say. Rhia nodded in agreement, though both were left wondering how it ever could be. He reached out and held her hand for comfort.

They stood holding hands, silently absorbing the scene unfolding before them, as they inched closer to the ticket counter. Richard had shoved his identification and more than enough money to cover whatever the tickets would cost into a pocket of his worn-out jeans so as not to have to open a briefcase full of money in a room full of desperate people, Rhia had tucked hers into the external pocket of his backpack. When they were almost to the counter, they both dug them out to make the purchase as quick as possible. Once it was their turn, they stepped up to the counter trying to look as casual as the circumstance allowed.

The aging woman behind the counter was noticeably overwhelmed by the overall chaos of the morning which, to her, had come with next to no warning. Before either of them could say anything, the woman spoke up with a disclaimer that was clearly the result of already having had to repeat herself more times today than she was used to in a year; "I ask you in advance for your patience, our computer system is not what it used to be and the unusual volume today has it almost at a standstill. Please understand that many departure times are already sold out and you are unlikely to get to a specific location without significant wait times and layovers due to anticipated delays."

Rhia took charge of speaking with the woman, "That is quite alright. We are not set on any destination; we are only looking to get out before the fighting gets worse." The woman looked relieved to not have to hear a plea as to why they needed to go to a specific place at a specific time.

Her fingers clacked on her keyboard and said, as much to herself as the two of them, "That is all anyone can hope for at this point." The old computer was obviously taking its time, so to get ahead of the next step she asked them for identification. They handed theirs over for her to merely skim them and hand them back.

"Trying to enter an actual name on the ticket is just asking for the system to crash," the woman said in an attempt to make conversation as the system took its time. After a few moments another screen must have popped up because she listed off several cities and departure times (all well into the afternoon). Richard and

Rhia must have looked visibly disappointed to have to wait several hours to leave because she reassured them, "You two are actually lucky, there are already people towards the back of the line who will have to wait until tomorrow...if we are even running by then." The frustrated railway ticket worker act she had been putting on faded for a second, replaced by the knowing human being faced with the near certain reality that she would not end up on any of the trains that she was selling tickets to.

"Whichever leaves the soonest will work just fine," said Rhia, softening her voice to be as soothing as it could.

The computer was at a standstill as the woman clicked several times out of frustration before continuing the conversation, "It's been like this all morning. It will just take a few minutes to load." Richard and Rhia stood with sincere patience and sympathy for her. To pass the time and change the conversation about the grim world waiting outside of the train station, the woman asked; "You two are younger than most who have come through today, are you two newlyweds off on an unplanned honeymoon?"

Both Richard and Rhia blushed awkwardly and giggled at the unexpected normalcy of her question, "No, nothing like that."

"Well, what are you waiting for? There isn't much time to waste all things considered." She looked directly at Richard and offered maternal advice, "You'd be a fool to miss your chance with a pretty little thing like her. She obviously loves you enough to run off with you, the least you can do is make it official." The pair were warmed by her words, momentarily distracting them from what was going on around them.

The woman could see the two of them relaxing in front of her in real time and, with the computer yet to respond, kept the conversation going; "I'm not so lucky. Lucky enough that I have food and a job and a place to live, but I was busy taking care of my parents when I was your age. Working and tending to their health when I should have been out catching the eye of a handsome young thing like him."

Richard had a sudden idea and asked her, "You don't have anyone waiting behind for you in the city?"

"Can't say that I do. I go out for a drink every so often with some of the people I work with, but we all have our own lives. If I'm being honest, I was never much into handsome young lads like you even when I was your age–if you catch my meaning," she said more as a matter of fact than as a topic of remorse.

Richard pulled out all of the money he had stuffed into his pocket and laid it on the counter, "If it isn't too late, I'd like to buy three tickets. Two on the first train out of here and one to wherever you want to go. You can keep the rest and leave the city before it is too late."

She looked across the ticket desk at him, completely stunned by the show of generosity. Wheels in her head began turning as she contemplated being able to get out of the city before she was trapped. It wasn't relief on her face though, both Rhia and Richard could see she was weighing the same feelings as most of the people in the line (themselves included)–the prospect of having to leave behind everything they had ever known.

"I thank you for the offer young man, I really do. As much as I would like to get away from the unpleasant business going on out there, it wouldn't be right of me to leave with all of these people trying to get their tickets. It's not a glamorous job, but this computer system is finicky and hard to operate. If my coworkers and I up and left, the transit authority would have a terrible time trying to replace us in the middle of all of this, and then nobody would be able to leave the city."

In that moment Richard saw a whole different meaning to the word duty than he had ever considered in his entire life. Duty to the system didn't necessarily have to have the ruthless productivity-oriented meaning that his college had spent so many years trying to drill into his head, nor was benevolent adherence to duty limited to acting on behalf of a greater morally justified cause. Here was an average woman, doing her duty to the system, but doing it because it was the one small way she could help the people in the world around her.

The computer must have unfrozen, because she picked up a few bills from the stack he had sat on the counter and pushed the remainder back towards him. Before he could protest, she put the bills in her drawer, grabbed his change, and tore the newly printed tickets from their printer. She laid the tickets and his change on top of the stack of money he still hadn't grabbed.

He picked the pile up as she said, "Thank you both for making my day a little less stressful. I wish you both safe travels. Take my advice young man and make an honest woman out of her, you two make a handsome couple." Richard and Rhia were both emotional as they thanked her and made their way towards the platform staging area. The woman looked at them tenderly for one last moment before dawning her frustrated railway worker persona and yelling out, "next."

The security line was moving considerably faster than the ticket line because the people manning it were every bit as flustered at the surge of people as the aging woman behind the ticket counter had pretended to be. Both Rhia and Richard were doing their best to look composed, but it hardly mattered as everyone in the whole station was acting frantic. It had taken well over an hour to get their tickets and the gunshots in the distance were becoming much more frequent, at times overlapping and lasting for longer and longer. What was playing out on the streets was no longer a series of skirmishes, it had become a full-on battle.

When it was their turn to be checked by security, the man just mimed setting their bags down and taking off a backpack. Rhia and Richard quickly did as prompted. The man ran a metal detector over the backpack and bag, picked the briefcase up and ran the metal detector over the middle of it, before finally doing a lackluster pass over both of their bodies before unceremoniously waving them through. They grabbed their things and hurried into the waiting area to await their train.

There was still a decent amount of time before they would depart, so the two of them found a spot against a wall (out of the way of what seemed to be the main walkway of the waiting area). Once they were seated, Rhia leaned her head on his shoulder and they watched the frantic people count down the seconds until their departures in silence. Even with the murmur of voices bouncing off the walls, the fighting in the distance could still be clearly heard. Not only were the gunshots becoming almost non-stop, they were punctuated at intervals by the sound of small explosions. There was little that anyone in the station could do to escape thinking about what was quickly turning from a battle into a war.

The sounds of the fighting were enough to get to anyone, but Richard and Rhia felt their stomachs tighten every time they heard an explosion because they knew very well that people that they knew and loved were the targets. In all his years at his middle management school he had only known it to be the home of a bunch of overprivileged unthinking drones-in-training, but he sat there now imagining the campus that he had so deeply resented as the battlefield that it had become. The hostility he had harbored for so many years against his 'peers' had melted away, replaced by sympathy for their naivety going up in the flames of the explosions now wracking the city.

Rhia had heard her father talk about war her entire life. He was careful never to glorify it and censored only what was absolutely necessary to spare his audience. As she had gotten older, she had become privy to his full descriptions of all of the hellish things it entailed. Mangled bodies, blood lust, rape, and murder were the norm rather than the exception. Worse than the uncensored understanding of what was taking place was knowing that her father and brother were now at ground zero for where it would all happen. Her father had survived war before and had survived the many physical and emotional scars with his sanity intact. For all of her brother's bravado, he was now in the middle of something that exceeded imagination and even if he managed to survive it there was no guarantee his mind would.

She looked up at Richard. The last 12 hours had been so surreal she had not even stopped to think about how strange it was to be sitting here with a young man she had accidentally crashed out of the sky onto just months ago. Before she had met Richard, her world was full of the lavish life contained in the walls of her father's manor-a life that was so false behind its ornate trappings that she had done anything she could just to escape from it. Here she sat, fully steeped in a life so real that the pain of it had dulled her ability to enjoy it. She had known, at least as a matter of intellectual curiosity, that the comforts of life had a way of blinding a person--now she understood that the pain of reality could be equally blinding.

Rhia knew that there would always be a part of her, regardless of the outcome of their cause and even if her father and brother both survived unscathed, that would regret having left them to the gunfire sounding in the distance. Still, as she looked at Richard, she took comfort that she was in good company. His haphazardly-rugged angst that had peaked her initial curiosity had morphed into the chiseled hardening of a young man with something to lose. The passion and purpose suited him.

She had grown too. The girl in her that never felt at home playing dress up for the awkward and uninteresting boys paraded in front of her by the important people in her father's orbit had given way to a young woman who knew she had no small part to play in the shaping of the world to come, with the utmost confidence in her ability to play it. She loved that Richard, rather than feeling insecure about her increasing outward confidence, seemed to gravitate to her harder and harder the more she grew into herself. They were all that each other had for the foreseeable future and she, in that moment—sitting on the wall of a railway station while the city they knew and grew up in went up in flames, couldn't have imagined a better person to be stuck with.

As the day dragged on, Richard watched as the people who had arrived before them boarded their respective trains and left the city. When each new train arrived, it brought a short-lived wave of excitement from the now-refugees waiting their turn. When the full trains would depart, the excitement quickly evaporated into worry that it would be the last one and that they would all be stuck so close to escaping. As much as he liked to think he was different from the average person, he too could feel excitement and despair tugging and pulling at him like the tides.

Delays had pushed their departure further and further back. The railway workers had stopped allowing people through the lines hours ago and Richard could see that hundreds of people had chosen to camp in the entrance for the evening to try and get a ticket in the morning. The security workers were now just manning a portable metal barricade they had placed to block the way to the waiting area.

Every few hours, armed police had made walkthroughs of the waiting crowd. It had been quite some time since Richard had seen a police officer, they mostly only kept visible patrols in areas inhabited by the wealthy and rarely ventured to his normal stomping grounds outside of extreme circumstances, and he couldn't help but think that they didn't look as menacing as his memory made them out to be. The way that they made a show of looking around rather than actually looking around, coupled with a visible and humanizing look of unease when the sound of fighting in the distance would crescendo with a burst of explosions, suggested that they were as unhappy with the situation as anyone else.

In a weird way it made sense to Richard that they were more restrained and human than the Citizens Watchers who governed through terror in poorer districts in their absence, after all-the Citizens Watch was populated by people morally and mentally unfit to represent formal law enforcement. The evidence worn onto their visibly worried faces that even badge carrying members of the system's enforcement had no vested interest in risking their necks to uphold it was a hopeful sight. In the hours immediately after Mark and the others had fallen in a haze of bullets the whole system they had been trying to spite seemed invincible, but here was proof that at least parts of it were vulnerable to basic human fear and compassion.

He looked down at Rhia, nestled comfortably in the crook of his arm. They had made sporadic conversation as the day wore its way into the afternoon, but neither of them could speak openly about what was on their mind for fear of being overheard. He was acutely aware that he would find little sympathy in a room full of scared refugees for his or his friends' actions, actions that had been the catalyst for the people now anxiously waiting in the station needing to leave their entire lives behind. Even with the despair hanging so thick in the air (and the pain of losing Mark that he had put on pause until he found a more appropriate opportunity to grieve), he couldn't help but be grateful when he looked down at the beautiful and vibrant girl with stars in her eyes. The miserable world had taken nearly everything that he had ever cared about, but here at what seemed like the end of all things was a magnificent young woman with more fire and passion than anyone he had ever met.

There was nothing about their current situation that made him think for a second that the task in front of them would be easy. As much as he had paid very close attention to anything and everything that Gergory had said or done, there were still many things he would have to practice before he could ever hope to fill Gregory's massive shoes. The ease at which Gregory could recruit people to his cause was a natural born gift that Richard knew he would spend his whole life practicing just to make a passable imitation of. Rhia was extremely gifted too. As he ran his fingers through her hair, he was certain that she could handle whatever came next and took comfort that there was nobody else in the world he would rather face it with.

Chapter 34

The shadows cast by the light from the windows of the building had grown long and night was quickly approaching. Hours upon hours of hearing the battle raging outside in the streets had taken a heavy toll on the anxious mob fleeing the city. Early in the day people had kept up conversations, like whistling in the dark, to keep the terrifying reality of the world around them at bay. Now, people sat nearly silently (some crying, some praying, some faking patience) with nothing to do but wait.

Rhia and Richard were feeling the fatigue of their last few weeks on top of the tension of the situation, but they had higher hopes than many of the people around them as they were set to board the next train that arrived.

The closer it got, the more anxious they felt. In the hurry

to get to the station, neither had considered what they would do for food. Luckily for the two of them, the station had a built-in commissary. By the time they realized they would need food at some point in the journey, neither had been remotely hungry following the events of the previous evening, the commissary had been nearly picked through. They grabbed handfuls of the remaining food and stood in line to check out.

While they were waiting, Rhia said; "Keep track of what it costs and make sure you take half of it out of what my father gave me."

Richard was taken aback by her concern. He hadn't even considered dividing the contents of the briefcase into his and hers. As far as he was concerned, he hadn't done anything to deserve more of a claim to its contents than she had.

"I appreciate the thought, but the task ahead of us isn't *my* task or *your* task–it's *our* task. Our task, our money."

She dawned an indignant look in protest, "I know it's our task, but I don't want to feel like some trophy wife. I spent my whole life surrounded by the important people in my fathers' world and I always swore that I wouldn't end up at the financial mercy of a man like so many of the women in that world."

Richard had a moment to think about what she had said because it was their turn to pay. The cashier looked as exhausted as they felt and wasted no time getting them rung up and paid. Both Richard and Rhia felt the urge to strike up some type of conversation with the tired worker as they checked out, but the enormity of what was going on around them left them at a loss for words.

They didn't return to where they had been seated against the wall as their train was expected to arrive very soon, but rather found a spot to stand closer to where the person would check their ticket and let them outside onto the platform.

Before Rhia could start up the conversation again, Richard wrapped his arms around her and spoke in a hushed voice, "I can't argue with your reasoning and I understand that it is important, but right now the only thing that matters is that we are here for each other. Once we are far enough away to have this conversation in safety, I'm all ears. Right now, I'm holding on because I know that I'll be alright as long as we're in this together." His voice was thick with the type of emotion that conveyed how much everything that had happened had broken him, more than his words could ever explain.

As she wrapped her arms around him and squeezed back, she considered how he must be feeling. She was worried because her father and brother *might* die. There was no uncertainty for Richard. His family was dead, his best friend was dead, and he too was worried about the last few people (other than herself) dying as well. It was entirely possible that she would see her loved ones again, Richard had no such hope outside of being reunited with them in death.

They might have stood there embracing forever, but just then it was announced that their train had arrived at long last. Neither could hide their relief and excitement. Rhia reached up and pulled his head in for a passionate kiss before the two of them made sure they had their few remaining belongings in order to board without issue. They could see the train coming to a stop outside.

Like everything else that day, the process of showing their tickets and boarding the train was fairly easy-especially considering they were easily carrying everything they were bringing with them. In a few short minutes they had already made their way to their seats and watched out the window as the remaining lucky passengers did the same. They grabbed each other's hands and breathed their first real sigh of relief in nearly 24 hours.

Outside the building, the explosions in the city sounded more menacing. Gunfire had dwindled since the height of the day, but explosions were becoming more frequent. Everyone in the car with them waited on bated breath for the train to begin rolling them onwards towards safety. The desperation that weighed so heavy inside the station was replaced by gratitude and tentative optimism. When the train lurched into motion, there were muffled cheers throughout the train car.

As the train departed the station, Rhia stared out the window at the now setting sun. She knew that it was the same dull sunset of recent years that she had watched so many times before, but it seemed more beautiful than anytime she could remember. Even with the worry for her brother and father as well as the sadness of the loss of her friends and companions fresh in her mind, she knew that there was reason to hope for the future. The dull sun wasn't setting on her love for the people in her life nor her dreams for a new world and a better tomorrow. It was setting on the cruel, unjust, dishonest, nightmare from which she had always wanted to escape.

Once the train had finally gotten up to speed and the city was in the process of fading to memory behind her, she leaned over on Richard and let herself begin to doze off. In spite of everything that had happened and would happen, she was happy that her life was finally in her own hands.

Richard felt her lean on him as he watched out the window as darkness enveloped the city speeding by them. They were already far enough away and the train was loud enough that he could no longer hear explosions, though he could still see the flashes they created in the distance. He felt her breathing becoming more rhythmic as she drifted off to sleep. His own eyes were growing heavy, but he was intent on seeing the last of the city fade from his view. The entire world as he had known it was rapidly disappearing into the distance.

Sleep was near, but he couldn't help wondering why any of it had happened. Memories of the last few months whirled through his head; his nighttime adventures with Mark, Gregory's charismatic speeches and the electricity he had brought into the world around him, Old Dirge's bizarre life finally giving way to a purpose, and meeting the beautiful and brilliant girl now fast asleep on his shoulder. Recent memories combined with the memories of his childhood and his parents. He remembered the letter from his father that he hadn't had the resolve to open tucked into his backpack.

As slowly and gently as he could so as not to wake Rhia; he unzipped the pocket, dug the letter out, and opened it.

"Dear Richard,

I wish that I could have delivered this to you in person, but I fear that my days are numbered as I find that I am ready to be reunited with your mother. My friend has assured me that he will do his best to care for you, so I hope that this letter finds you well.

Over my years of confinement, I have often wondered if the price you and your mother had to pay for my optimism was worth it. It is a matter of debate in my mind that I have come to understand that I cannot answer. In the end, my opinion from the inside of a cell means little. You, Richard, are the only one who can answer that question.

I was not content to leave a world for you devoid of the joys and freedoms that the generations before you enjoyed without a second thought. Everything I did, and the whole mess that came from it, I did out of love for you and a hope that you may live to see a better future. It has always been the way of change that some have to pay a heavier price than others and I am sorry I left you no choice in the price you were to pay.

Just know that wherever you go and whatever you decide to make of your life, that I will always love you.

-See you on the other side, Dad."

Silent tears streamed down Richard's face. He never had the opportunity to become educated like his father nor have the unencumbered life experiences that his father had, but here he sat with the same question his father had gone to the grave without an answer to—*was it all worth it?*

Richard knew enough scattered history to know he and his friends were not the first to rebel against an unjust system. He had understood enough of what his father had said in his childhood and what Gregory had explained in recent months that he knew something absolutely had to be done. The sorrow he felt for the loss of Mark, the sorrow he and his mother had carried for years at the loss of his father, and the sorrow he was already too callous to add to his conscious when he lost his mother were just the price that some humans had to pay from time to time when the world got bad enough.

There didn't have to be a cosmic reason for it. The world had gotten so bad for so many that the misfortune which had plagued his existence was just dealt by the lottery of life. Mark paid with his life, but if it hadn't been Mark it would just have been someone else somewhere at some time. The only blame people like himself, Rhia, Gregory, and his father were responsible for was the crime of caring about what kind of world they lived in. They couldn't wish away the way they felt any more than they could make a wish, snap their fingers, and hope the world would magically transform into a more hospitable place.

They couldn't just sit idly by. The suffering in the world was worse than the suffering that it would take to change it, so they had started a revolution. He already missed Mark more than he could fully process, but he knew that countless people who would never know Mark's name would live better lives if they could successfully wrestle change from the deadly grip of the system. As long as humans lived together, there would always be need for growth and change. If people put off growth and change for too long, it would always lead to some paying the ultimate price for it. This time was just his turn to pay three times over.

The tears had stopped and he looked down at Rhia with more certainty than he had ever felt in his life. They would do whatever it took to make sure that price wasn't paid in vain. Even with all the tragedy they were leaving further and further behind in the distance-there they sat, with more hope than he had ever thought was possible. It was dark and he closed his eyes.